PRINCE NORODOM SIHANOUK

PRINCE NORODOM SIHANOUK

Madhavi Kuckreja

CHELSEA HOUSE PUBLISHERS
NEW YORK
PHILADELPHIA

Chelsea House Publishers
EDITOR-IN-CHIEF: Nancy Toff
EXECUTIVE EDITOR: Remmel T. Nunn
MANAGING EDITOR: Karyn Gullen Browne
COPY CHIEF: Juliann Barbato
PICTURE EDITOR: Adrian G. Allen
ART DIRECTOR: Maria Epes
MANUFACTURING MANAGER: Gerald Levine

World Leaders—Past & Present
SENIOR EDITOR: John W. Selfridge

Staff for PRINCE NORODOM SIHANOUK
ASSOCIATE EDITOR: Jeff Klein
COPY EDITOR: Richard Klin
DEPUTY COPY CHIEF: Mark Rifkin
EDITORIAL ASSISTANT: Nate Eaton
PICTURE RESEARCHER: Leslie Seldin
ASSISTANT ART DIRECTOR: Loraine Machlin
DESIGNER: David Murray
ASSISTANT DESIGNER: James Baker
PRODUCTION MANAGER: Joseph Romano
PRODUCTION COORDINATOR: Marie Claire Cebrián
COVER ILLUSTRATION: Vilma Ortiz

First Printing

1 3 5 7 9 8 6 4 2

Library of Congress Cataloging-in-Publication Data

Kuckreja, Madhavi.
    Prince Norodom Sihanouk/Madhavi Kuckreja.
    p.   cm.—(World leaders past & present)
    Includes bibliographical references.
    Summary: A biography of the Cambodian head of state who was
overthrown in 1970.
    ISBN 1-55546-851-9
          0-7910-0686-7 (pbk.)
    1. Norodom Sihanouk, Prince, 1922–   —Juvenile literature.
2. Cambodia—Kings and rulers—Biography—Juvenile literature. [1.
Norodom Sihanouk, Prince, 1922–   . 2. Heads of state. 3.
Cambodia—History] I. Title. II. Series.
DS554.83.N6K83   1990
959.604′092—dc20   89–48914
[B]   CIP
[92]   AC

Contents

John Adams
John Quincy Adams
Konrad Adenauer
Alexander the Great
Salvador Allende
Marc Antony
Corazon Aquino
Yasir Arafat
King Arthur
Hafez al-Assad
Kemal Atatürk
Attila
Clement Attlee
Augustus Caesar
Menachem Begin
David Ben-Gurion
Otto von Bismarck
Léon Blum
Simon Bolívar
Cesare Borgia
Willy Brandt
Leonid Brezhnev
Julius Caesar
John Calvin
Jimmy Carter
Fidel Castro
Catherine the Great
Charlemagne
Chiang Kai-Shek
Winston Churchill
Georges Clemenceau
Cleopatra
Constantine the Great
Hernán Cortés
Oliver Cromwell
Georges-Jacques
   Danton
Jefferson Davis
Moshe Dayan
Charles de Gaulle
Eamon De Valera
Eugene Debs
Deng Xiaoping
Benjamin Disraeli
Alexander Dubček
François & Jean-Claude
   Duvalier
Dwight Eisenhower
Eleanor of Aquitaine
Elizabeth I
Faisal
Ferdinand & Isabella
Francisco Franco
Benjamin Franklin

Frederick the Great
Indira Gandhi
Mohandas Gandhi
Giuseppe Garibaldi
Amin & Bashir Gemayel
Genghis Khan
William Gladstone
Mikhail Gorbachev
Ulysses S. Grant
Ernesto "Che" Guevara
Tenzin Gyatso
Alexander Hamilton
Dag Hammarskjöld
Henry VIII
Henry of Navarre
Paul von Hindenburg
Hirohito
Adolf Hitler
Ho Chi Minh
King Hussein
Ivan the Terrible
Andrew Jackson
James I
Wojciech Jaruzelski
Thomas Jefferson
Joan of Arc
Pope John XXIII
Pope John Paul II
Lyndon Johnson
Benito Juárez
John Kennedy
Robert Kennedy
Jomo Kenyatta
Ayatollah Khomeini
Nikita Khrushchev
Kim Il Sung
Martin Luther King, Jr.
Henry Kissinger
Kublai Khan
Lafayette
Robert E. Lee
Vladimir Lenin
Abraham Lincoln
David Lloyd George
Louis XIV
Martin Luther
Judas Maccabeus
James Madison
Nelson & Winnie
   Mandela
Mao Zedong
Ferdinand Marcos
George Marshall

Mary, Queen of Scots
Tomáš Masaryk
Golda Meir
Klemens von Metternich
James Monroe
Hosni Mubarak
Robert Mugabe
Benito Mussolini
Napoléon Bonaparte
Gamal Abdel Nasser
Jawaharlal Nehru
Nero
Nicholas II
Richard Nixon
Kwame Nkrumah
Daniel Ortega
Mohammed Reza Pahlavi
Thomas Paine
Charles Stewart
   Parnell
Pericles
Juan Perón
Peter the Great
Pol Pot
Muammar el-Qaddafi
Ronald Reagan
Cardinal Richelieu
Maximilien Robespierre
Eleanor Roosevelt
Franklin Roosevelt
Theodore Roosevelt
Anwar Sadat
Haile Selassie
Prince Sihanouk
Jan Smuts
Joseph Stalin
Sukarno
Sun Yat-sen
Tamerlane
Mother Teresa
Margaret Thatcher
Josip Broz Tito
Toussaint L'Ouverture
Leon Trotsky
Pierre Trudeau
Harry Truman
Queen Victoria
Lech Walesa
George Washington
Chaim Weizmann
Woodrow Wilson
Xerxes
Emiliano Zapata
Zhou Enlai

CHELSEA HOUSE PUBLISHERS

ON LEADERSHIP

Arthur M. Schlesinger, jr.

LEADERSHIP, it may be said, is really what makes the world go round. Love no doubt smooths the passage; but love is a private transaction between consenting adults. Leadership is a public transaction with history. The idea of leadership affirms the capacity of individuals to move, inspire, and mobilize masses of people so that they act together in pursuit of an end. Sometimes leadership serves good purposes, sometimes bad; but whether the end is benign or evil, great leaders are those men and women who leave their personal stamp on history.

Now, the very concept of leadership implies the proposition that individuals can make a difference. This proposition has never been universally accepted. From classical times to the present day, eminent thinkers have regarded individuals as no more than the agents and pawns of larger forces, whether the gods and goddesses of the ancient world or, in the modern era, race, class, nation, the dialectic, the will of the people, the spirit of the times, history itself. Against such forces, the individual dwindles into insignificance.

So contends the thesis of historical determinism. Tolstoy's great novel *War and Peace* offers a famous statement of the case. Why, Tolstoy asked, did millions of men in the Napoleonic Wars, denying their human feelings and their common sense, move back and forth across Europe slaughtering their fellows? "The war," Tolstoy answered, "was bound to happen simply because it was bound to happen." All prior history predetermined it. As for leaders, they, Tolstoy said, "are but the labels that serve to give a name to an end and, like labels, they have the least possible connection with the event." The greater the leader, "the more conspicuous the inevitability and the predestination of every act he commits." The leader, said Tolstoy, is "the slave of history."

Determinism takes many forms. Marxism is the determinism of class. Nazism the determinism of race. But the idea of men and women as the slaves of history runs athwart the deepest human instincts. Rigid determinism abolishes the idea of human freedom—

the assumption of free choice that underlies every move we make, every word we speak, every thought we think. It abolishes the idea of human responsibility, since it is manifestly unfair to reward or punish people for actions that are by definition beyond their control. No one can live consistently by any deterministic creed. The Marxist states prove this themselves by their extreme susceptibility to the cult of leadership.

More than that, history refutes the idea that individuals make no difference. In December 1931 a British politician crossing Park Avenue in New York City between 76th and 77th Streets around 10:30 P.M. looked in the wrong direction and was knocked down by an automobile—a moment, he later recalled, of a man aghast, a world aglare: "I do not understand why I was not broken like an eggshell or squashed like a gooseberry." Fourteen months later an American politician, sitting in an open car in Miami, Florida, was fired on by an assassin; the man beside him was hit. Those who believe that individuals make no difference to history might well ponder whether the next two decades would have been the same had Mario Constasino's car killed Winston Churchill in 1931 and Giuseppe Zangara's bullet killed Franklin Roosevelt in 1933. Suppose, in addition, that Adolf Hitler had been killed in the street fighting during the Munich *Putsch* of 1923 and that Lenin had died of typhus during World War I. What would the 20th century be like now?

For better or for worse, individuals do make a difference. "The notion that a people can run itself and its affairs anonymously," wrote the philosopher William James, "is now well known to be the silliest of absurdities. Mankind does nothing save through initiatives on the part of inventors, great or small, and imitation by the rest of us—these are the sole factors in human progress. Individuals of genius show the way, and set the patterns, which common people then adopt and follow."

Leadership, James suggests, means leadership in thought as well as in action. In the long run, leaders in thought may well make the greater difference to the world. But, as Woodrow Wilson once said, "Those only are leaders of men, in the general eye, who lead in action. . . . It is at their hands that new thought gets its translation into the crude language of deeds." Leaders in thought often invent in solitude and obscurity, leaving to later generations the tasks of imitation. Leaders in action—the leaders portrayed in this series—have to be effective in their own time.

Leaders have done great harm to the world. They have also conferred great benefits. You will find both sorts in this series. Even "good" leaders must be regarded with a certain wariness. Leaders are not demigods; they put on their trousers one leg after another just like ordinary mortals. No leader is infallible, and every leader needs to be reminded of this at regular intervals. Irreverence irritates leaders but is their salvation. Unquestioning submission corrupts leaders and demeans followers. Making a cult of a leader is always a mistake. Fortunately hero worship generates its own antidote. "Every hero," said Emerson, "becomes a bore at last."

The signal benefit the great leaders confer is to embolden the rest of us to live according to our own best selves, to be active, insistent, and resolute in affirming our own sense of things. For great leaders attest to the reality of human freedom against the supposed inevitabilities of history. And they attest to the wisdom and power that may lie within the most unlikely of us, which is why Abraham Lincoln remains the supreme example of great leadership. A great leader, said Emerson, exhibits new possibilities to all humanity. "We feed on genius. . . . Great men exist that there may be greater men."

Great leaders, in short, justify themselves by emancipating and empowering their followers. So humanity struggles to master its destiny, remembering with Alexis de Tocqueville: "It is true that around every man a fatal circle is traced beyond which he cannot pass; but within the wide verge of that circle he is powerful and free; as it is with man, so with communities."

1

The Abdication

Nothing like it had ever happened in the long history of Cambodia, a small country tucked away inside the peninsula of Southeast Asia. On March 2, 1955, the regular programming of Cambodia's national radio was interrupted for a special announcement from the country's 32-year-old ruler, King Norodom Sihanouk. Wherever there was a radio to be heard — in the stylish, palm-shaded homes of the aristocracy, in the bustling cafés and shops of Phnom Penh, the capital city, and in army barracks, government offices, and village headmen's huts across the land — people stopped what they were doing and listened in alarm and excitement to the voice of their king.

Sihanouk told the Cambodian people that he had decided to do something that no Cambodian king had ever done — to abdicate the throne. Although he had reigned as king of Cambodia since the age of 18, he was now stepping down. Though he would retain the title of prince, he would no longer be the country's head of state. That position would be filled by the new king, who was none other than Sihanouk's elderly father, Norodom Suramarit.

We had been at peace because of one man, Norodom Sihanouk. The French appointed him king when he was a schoolboy, expecting that he would be easy to control, but Sihanouk outmaneuvered them, just as he outmaneuvered everyone else.
—HAING NGOR
Cambodian refugee

Prince Norodom Sihanouk speaks to a crowd in October 1955, seven months after he gave up the throne of Cambodia to run in the Southeast Asian nation's first election. The 32-year-old Sihanouk was already credited with having gained Cambodia's independence from France in 1954.

Sihanouk's father, Norodom Suramarit, who became king when Sihanouk abdicated in March 1955. Here King Suramarit and Sihanouk's mother, Queen Kossamak, prepare to receive guests after the coronation ceremonies in Phnom Penh, the capital of Cambodia.

Sihanouk told the listening nation that Cambodia's political situation made it necessary for him to abdicate the throne. Under the constitution that Cambodia had adopted just a few years earlier, in 1947, the king was not eligible to run for elected office or to participate in party politics. Sihanouk explained that because he wished to serve the Cambodians as a party official, he found it necessary to step down. By the time the broadcast ended, something very basic to Cambodian life and culture had changed forever. The king — who was called Royal Father by most Cambodians and was believed by many of them to be a god—was the king no longer.

Norodom Sihanouk has played a central role in Cambodian politics since his childhood. He has been prince, king, prime minister, foreign minister, head of state, president, refugee, political prisoner, and freedom fighter. Yet perhaps no other event in his long and eventful political life more clearly shows his rare combination of shrewdness and idealistic vision than his abdication of the throne. At a troubled moment in Cambodia's history, Sihanouk was wise enough to see that the political power of the future would lie not with the country's age-old tradition of absolute rule by the king but with the more modern ideas of representative government to which many of the younger Cambodians had been exposed. And he was shrewd enough to realize that in order to continue to wield power, he would have to make a great leap from the hereditary throne to the elected legislature. In a way, Sihanouk's transformation of himself from king to party politician paralleled the sweeping changes that were overtaking Cambodia itself as the country was transformed — painfully at times — from a quaint colonial backwater ornamented with the relics of an ancient monarchy into a modern nation-state.

Where radios did not exist, the news of King Sihanouk's abdication was carried rapidly by word of mouth. Within a week or so, even many of the tribespeople called the Khmer Loeu, who lived in remote fastnesses in the jungle-covered hills in the northern and eastern parts of the country, had learned of it. The news was received with mixed feelings. It was not the first piece of unsettling news that the Cambodian people had had to digest. In fact, King Sihanouk's abdication was just one of many events that had shaken Cambodia out of its ancient orbit.

First had come the French. Advancing into Southeast Asia in the mid-19th century, French soldiers and statesmen gradually gained control of the kingdoms of Laos, Cambodia, and Vietnam, which in 1862 were merged together into a colonial possession called French Indochina. Although the French had been firmly established in Indochina for longer than Sihanouk or any of his subjects had been alive,

> *I am so antimilitary that when I became King and had to take courses at a military academy, I could barely tell the difference between a sergeant and a captain. . . . I am an artist. I was born an artist and what I like best is the cinema, music, literature.*
> —PRINCE NORODOM SIHANOUK
> in an interview
> with journalist
> Oriana Fallaci, 1973

15

they were still regarded as recent intruders, and resentment of French occupation was growing. And after the French came the Japanese. In their quest for Asian domination, Japanese troops had occupied Cambodia for several years during World War II.

The end of the war and the departure of the Japanese had not brought a return to the prewar way of life. The voices within Cambodia that were calling out for national independence had grown louder, and King Sihanouk's was one of the loudest of all. Only a year and a half before the abdication, in the autumn of 1953, Cambodia had received its independence from France after nearly a century of French domination, and both the supporters and the critics of King Sihanouk agreed that he deserved the chief credit for forcing France to grant independence. Since that time, many Cambodians had expected national elections to be held — elections in which the Cambodian people would vote to elect their leaders for the first time in their history. Meanwhile, however, King Sihanouk and several groups that opposed him were striving fiercely for political power and the people's loyalty.

King Sihanouk abdicated the throne and became Prince Sihanouk so that he could compete in the turbulent world of party politics that was being born in Cambodia. Yet he did not enter politics on equal terms with his competitors and opponents. He was a prince, after all — and to many people, he continued to be a king for whom they felt awe and reverence. He was still able to command the respect and obedience of millions of Cambodians, particularly rural peasants, because generations of their forebears had believed that the kings of Cambodia were semisacred beings called *deva-rajas*, or god-kings. To many of Sihanouk's fellow countrymen, a king remained a king whether he changed his title or not, and the new politics of Cambodia — complete with parties, elections, and officials — did not change their fundamental loyalty to the monarch. Due in large part to this loyalty, Prince Sihanouk easily won his first election and remained in control of the country, almost as powerful as the kings of old, for 15 years.

An ancestral prophecy predicts that one day the unfortunate Khmer people will be forced to choose between being eaten by tigers or swallowed by crocodiles. Today we are seeing that prophecy fulfilled in the most tragic way possible.
—PRINCE NORODOM SIHANOUK
in 1980

Yet further changes, and still more drastic ones, were in store for Cambodia. In the 1960s, the war in neighboring Vietnam began to spill across the border into Cambodia. Dissatisfaction with Sihanouk was on the rise, and his grip on the reins of power slipped. Then, between 1970 and 1979, Cambodia was convulsed by civil war and national tragedy on a scale almost unimaginable. In a single decade, three governments were overthrown in turn. After each overthrow, a new regime took control and attempted to reshape Cambodian politics and society. The most ambitious of these restructurings was carried out between 1975 and 1978 by Pol Pot, the dictatorial leader of the Communist forces known as the Khmer Rouge, who renamed the country Democratic Kampuchea and systematically slaughtered between 1 and 2 million of his fellow Cambodians in a holocaust that has been compared to Adolf Hitler's attempted extermination of the Jews during World War II.

A beaming Sihanouk is mobbed by an enthusiastic crowd as he arrives at a Buddhist temple in Phnom Penh in 1962. In keeping with the traditional Cambodian belief that the nation's kings are descendants of ancient gods, many Cambodians, particularly those in the countryside, believed that Sihanouk was a divine figure.

Fleeing refugees pass a victim of the fighting that wracked Cambodia in 1973. During the 1970s, the small nation was subjected to several invasions, massive aerial bombing, bloody civil war, and finally a regime that conducted one of history's most horrific mass slaughters, in which at least one out of every seven Cambodians was killed.

The horrors of the Pol Pot regime ended when Vietnam invaded Democratic Kampuchea, but peace and a unified government have not yet returned to Cambodia. At least four different political organizations, each with its own army, claim various territories within the country and are vying for total control. Even the country's name has become uncertain. The current central government, which was established by Vietnam after its overthrow of Democratic Kampuchea, is called the People's Republic of Kampuchea. But Prince Sihanouk, along with the United States and many other nations, rejects the name Kampuchea because of its association with Pol Pot and the Khmer Rouge and

continues to use the name Cambodia to refer to the country.

On the day of his abdication, King Sihanouk gave up the hollow illusion of power so that he could continue to wield real political clout. Thirty-five years later, Prince Sihanouk is a political exile, one of the leaders of an uneasy alliance of forces that hopes to topple the Vietnam-backed regime that now holds sway in Phnom Penh. He is still shrewd, still a visionary, still a nimble but unpredictable politician — and he is still, despite decades of turmoil, perhaps the only person who can serve as a symbol and a spokesman for Cambodia both at home and to the world.

2

The Land and People of Cambodia

To understand Sihanouk and his life, it is necessary to know something about his country. Cambodia is inhabited by about 7,250,000 people; 90 percent of them belong to the Southeast Asian ethnic group called Khmer, and the others are of Chinese, Vietnamese, Burmese, or mixed descent. Their principal language is Khmer, although French and Vietnamese are also spoken. The predominant religion of the country is Buddhism, but there are also Muslims, Roman Catholics, and followers of traditional spirit- and ancestor-worshiping religions. Cambodia has an area of 69,898 square miles (181,035 square kilometers). It consists of a moist, fertile, low-lying central plain surrounded by a rim of steep, rugged, jungle-covered mountain ranges. Cambodia is located in Southeast Asia on the eastern coast of the Gulf of Siam and shares common borders with Thailand on the west and northwest, Laos on the northeast, and Vietnam on the east.

When we started as a nation more than one thousand years ago, we had what Western scholars used to call god-kings, because the kings were then gods. They represented everything, including the gods, so everything was centered on the king. And I think that is one of the reasons why we were so strong, because the people united all around the king.
—PRINCE NORODOM SIHANOUK

A Cambodian peasant works a rice paddy along the banks of the Mekong River in 1960. A rich agricultural nation whose bountiful harvests easily fed its population, until the 1960s Cambodia had been a conservative country relatively untouched by modernity.

A Cambodian peasant villager wears a traditional head covering. Some 90 percent of Cambodia's 7 million people belong to the Khmer ethnic group. The remainder are of Chinese, Vietnamese, Burmese, or mixed descent.

Cambodia lies in Asia's subtropical zone. Like the other countries of Southeast Asia and southern Asia, it is dependent upon the monsoons, or seasonal rains, which are an important source of water. The Mekong River is Cambodia's largest and most important river. It flows south from China along the border between Thailand and Laos and then through Cambodia before crossing southern Vietnam to empty into the Gulf of Thailand. The Mekong is fed by snowmelt in the mountains of southwestern China and also by the monsoons, which deposit enormous quantities of rain on the region from May through October. By June, the monsoons empty so much rain into the catchment area of the river that the Mekong carries more water than its delta can drain into the gulf. As a result, the river actually backs up. The excess water is pushed upstream along a small river called the Tonle Sab, which flows through the capital, Phnom Penh, located on an intersection of the Mekong and the Tonle Sab. The Tonle Sab thus flows south into the Mekong for six months and north, or uphill, into a large lake called the Tonle Sap for the rest of the year. Generations of Cambodians believed this remarkable phenomenon to be due to the powers of their god-kings. Every year while he was king, Sihanouk encouraged this belief by holding a colorful ceremony on the banks of the Tonle Sab. At the moment when the flow of water reversed itself, he blessed the river, thus making it look as though he had brought about the change in the direction of the water's flow.

The importance of this switch in the river's flow — and the appearance of power it gave to the kings — stems from the fact that the inrush of water into the Tonle Sap each year nourishes one of the richest freshwater fisheries in the world and irrigates a lush, productive rice-growing area around the lake. Fish from the Tonle Sap and rice from the surrounding region are two of Cambodia's staple food sources. In linking his royal power with the river and the lake, Sihanouk was following an old tradition; from earliest times, the area around the Tonle Sap, at the center of present-day Cambodia, has been the heart of Cambodian kingship and culture.

Cambodia was first settled by peoples migrating in waves from two directions. From the north came Chinese and Tibetan nomads, and from the south came Indonesian and Malaysian settlers. By about 350 B.C., these various groups had met in Cambodia's central plain and begun to merge into new peoples and cultures. Chief among these new peoples was a group called the Khmer, who soon became the dominant force in the region. The Khmer were the ancestors of most present-day Cambodians.

In the 1st century A.D., the kingdom of Funan was founded by the Khmer, who borrowed the language, the Hindu religion, and the arts of India. These Indian influences were carried to Funan across the Bay of Bengal from India by traders, travelers, and monks in a process that scholars have called Indianization or Sanskritization (Sanskrit was the ancient form of the Hindi language). Much of this Indianization came about because of the travels of learned men, or Brahmans, from India who brought with them their religion, traditions, architecture, and even dress styles. It was so common for Brahmans to arrive in Cambodia from India that the legend of Cambodia's origin features one such Brahman. He was called Kaundinya.

A small fishing village on the shores of the Tonle Sap, a large lake in central Cambodia fed by the waters of the Mekong. The flow of water between the Mekong and the Tonle Sap, for centuries the backbone of the nation's irrigation networks and fisheries, was closely identified with the institution of Cambodian kingship.

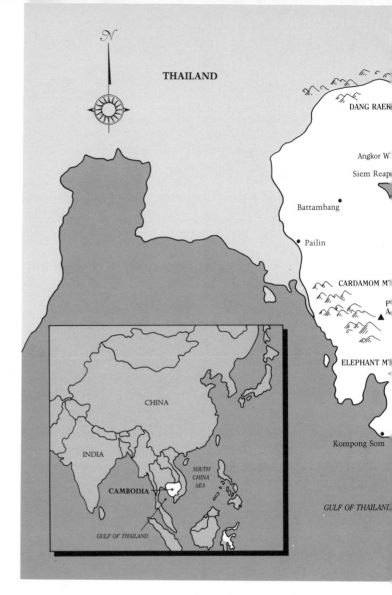

THAILAND

DANG RAEK

Angkor W

Siem Reap

Battambang

Pailin

CARDAMOM MT

ELEPHANT MT

Kompong Som

CHINA

INDIA

SOUTH
CHINA
SEA

CAMBODIA

GULF OF THAILAND

GULF OF THAILAND

A map of present-day Cambodia, a country the size of Missouri. For centuries, Cambodia has endured repeated invasions and occupations by its two larger and more powerful neighbors, Thailand and Vietnam. The most recent occupation, by Vietnam, began in 1979 and ended 10 years later.

Kaundinya was no ordinary Brahman. He possessed special powers. Having learned all he could from his guru, or teacher, he decided to travel to new lands to teach and also to learn from foreign cultures. He traveled for many months and finally reached the shores of Cambodia. As he approached the shore, a beautiful yet terrifying dragon-princess sailed toward him from the coast with a retinue of attendants. Kaundinya shot an arrow into her boat; this threw the boat off balance and threatened to capsize it. The princess was terrified by the power of the stranger and begged for mercy. Kaundinya

secured from her a promise to marry him. He then removed the arrow and boarded the princess's boat. As they approached another part of the shore, he saw that they were being received by the dragon-king himself. The marriage of Kaundinya and the princess was celebrated with elaborate ceremonies. He gave her priceless clothes and initiated her into the human way of life. In return, the dragon-king drank part of the sea and gave the new land that was revealed to Kaundinya. According to the legend, the new country that emerged when the dragon-king drained the sea was Cambodia.

For centuries the Indian influence remained strong in Cambodia; evidence of it can still be seen in the country's traditional architecture, customs, and religions. One of the most significant imports from India was the belief in a god-king. The concept of the deva-raja was the basis of the Cambodian way of life. The king was regarded as a manifestation of the Hindu god Vishnu, who is the Preserver of the Universe in the Hindu hierarchy of gods. To the common people of Cambodia, the king was therefore a larger-than-life figure. He was brave, intelligent, and just, and from him the people derived strength. To him, in turn, they owed complete obedience, and his power was absolute.

Funan prospered as a center of trade between India and China until about 550, when it was overcome by Chenla, another Khmer state located to the north, in what is now Thailand. Chenla, in turn, grew strong for several centuries and then disintegrated into many small, warring states. In the 8th century, Khmer princes who had been living on the island of Java in present-day Indonesia returned to Cambodia and founded a powerful new state that they called Kambuja. This state was the direct ancestor of modern Cambodia and Kampuchea (both names are versions of Kambuja).

Kambuja swiftly became the heart of a vast network of conquered and subject territories known as the Khmer Empire. The Khmer Empire dominated Southeast Asia for centuries. At the height of its power, around the year 1200, it controlled much of present-day Thailand, Laos, Vietnam, and Malaysia, as well as Cambodia itself.

At an early point in the empire's history, around the end of the 9th century, King Yasovarman I established his royal court in the region called Angkor, near the shores of the Tonle Sap (today this province of Cambodia is called Siem Reap). Angkor became the center of Cambodian government and culture, especially after the year 1130, when a great temple to the Hindu gods was built there by King Suryavarman II to commemorate his victory over the Chams, as the people of southern Vietnam were called.

Sihanouk had inherited a country filled with a sense of doom, a people who felt their race threatened by ambitious neighbors, and whose culture had reached a zenith centuries earlier. Because of history and inclination, the Cambodians allowed Sihanouk to provide them "shelter," to treat them like children hidden away in a tropical garden.

—ELIZABETH BECKER
American journalist

Around this time, an important change was taking place throughout Khmer society. Hinduism was being replaced by Buddhism, the second of the two great world religions to come out of India. By the time of Angkor's most glorious ruler, King Jayavarman VII, who reigned in the late 12th and early 13th centuries, Buddhism had become the dominant religion of the land and was declared by the kings to be the official, or state, religion. To mark this change, Jayavarman placed a gigantic stone image of the Buddha in the central tower of Suryavarman's great temple at Angkor, a temple that had formerly been dedicated to Vishnu. The large temple, along with the host of smaller temples that surrounded it, became known as Angkor Wat (a *wat* is a Buddhist monastery or shrine).

Jayavarman, like Suryavarman, was victorious in battle over the Chams, who had begun to invade Angkor. To celebrate his victories, he constructed an enormous new capital city of palaces near Angkor Wat. He called it Angkor Thom (*thom* means "big") and surrounded it with thick stone walls and crocodile-filled moats. At the center of Angkor Thom he erected a towering monument called the Bayon, covered with 216 carved faces of the Buddha, gazing serenely in all directions. The Bayon is also ornamented with friezes, or carved panels, that give a detailed picture of daily life during the heyday of the Khmer Empire: women bargaining in marketplaces,

A scene from the *Ramayana*, an ancient Indian epic, is depicted in a stone carving in Cambodia's Angkor Wat temple complex. Early Cambodia, known as the Khmer Empire, was heavily influenced by both Indian and Chinese culture.

27

The ruins of the Bayon temple, part of the Angkor Wat temple complex. Bayon features 216 carved faces of the Indian philosopher and mystic Siddhartha Gautama, who founded Buddhism, a religion derived from Hinduism. Buddhism teaches that the self can be purified and the material world transcended through self-discipline and self-awareness.

fishermen sweeping the waters of the Tonle Sap with their nets, and children driving oxcarts much like those that can still be found on the rural roads of Cambodia.

The glory and power of the Khmer Empire declined during the 13th and 14th centuries, as two rival states, one on either side of Cambodia, gained strength. To the east was Annam, or northern Vietnam, and to the west was Siam, today known as Thailand. Both became powerful and warlike, and each in turn nibbled away at the Khmer territories. In 1431, the Siamese captured and looted the great complex of temples and palaces at Angkor. The Khmer people fled south and founded a new capital at the junction of the Mekong River and the Tonle Sab. They called it Phnom Penh. After the withdrawal of the Siamese troops, Angkor was abandoned. It was soon overgrown by the encroaching jungle and, in time, was all but forgotten.

"Caught between the tiger and the crocodile" is a traditional Cambodian phrase that is used when a person is faced with two alternatives, both unpleasant. It can also be used to describe Cambodia's history for the four centuries that followed the Siamese conquest of Angkor in 1431. During this period, Cambodia grew progressively smaller and weaker and was preyed upon by its two rapacious neighbors, Thailand and Vietnam — the tiger and the crocodile. Because Cambodia's own armies were not strong enough to defeat or even to defend against either Thailand or Vietnam, the kings of Cambodia were forced to ask for help and protection from their enemies. For example, King Chey Chetta II, who ruled Cambodia from 1618 to 1628, wanted to free his country from Siamese domination, so he asked Vietnam to support his claim for independence and even married a Vietnamese princess. Before long, however, he found himself forced to pay tribute to Vietnam and to permit Vietnamese settlement of part of his kingdom. His descendants grew tired of bowing to Vietnam and asked the Siamese to help them throw out the Vietnamese — only to lose two important northern provinces, Battambang and Siem Reap, to Thailand. Every time Vietnam launched an attack or an invasion, Cambodia sought aid from Thailand; and when Thailand attacked, Cambodia turned to Vietnam for help.

Such help did not come without cost. The rulers of Thailand and Vietnam demanded high payment for their protection — either cash, workers, or territory. These relentless demands continued to weaken Cambodia and render it still more dependent upon outside help. Sometimes Cambodia's payments to its powerful neighbors took the form of control over succession within the ruling family; for example, King Ang Eng came to the Cambodian throne in 1779 at age six, selected by Thai advisers to the Cambodian royal family. He was crowned not in Phnom Penh but in Bangkok, the capital of Thailand, an unmistakable signal that Cambodia had become a puppet kingdom under Thai control. His son and successor, Ang Chan, was also crowned in Bangkok. Soon after returning to Phnom Penh,

Filled with a deep sympathy for the good of the world, the king swore his oath: "All the beings who are plunged in the ocean of existence, may I draw them out by virtue of this good work. And may the kings of Cambodia who come after me, attached to goodness . . . attain with their wives, dignitaries and friends the place of deliverance where there is no more illness."
—inscription on a hospital built during the reign of King Jayavarman VII in the 12th and 13th centuries

An entrance to one of the main temples at Angkor Wat. Most of the temple complex, one of the world's great architectural achievements, was built in the 1100s. It was badly damaged during the warfare and chaos of the 1970s and 1980s.

however, he sought support from the Nguyen dynasty, the rulers of Vietnam. A Thai army drove Ang Chan from the throne for several months, but he regained it with help from a Vietnamese army. During the remainder of his rule, he was forced to pay tribute to both Thailand and Vietnam.

Increasingly helpless, Cambodia was little more than a battlefield on which its neighbors fought for supremacy. In 1833, the Thai army swept through Cambodia and into part of Vietnam. The enraged Vietnamese responded by invading Cambodia in full force to drive the Thais out. The following year, the Vietnamese named a Cambodian princess, one of Ang Chan's teenage daughters, queen of Cambodia. She had no real power, however, and occupied her throne only with the protection of the Vietnamese, who proceeded to tighten their control over Cambodia, with the goal of complete overlordship. Half a dozen years later, though, a rebellion by the Cambodian peasants, together with another invasion from Thailand, forced the Vietnamese to retreat. According to 19th-century chronicles, for three years no rice was planted, and the Cambodian people lived on grass and roots while the armies of Thailand and

Vietnam surged back and forth across their land. Finally, in 1846, Thailand and Vietnam grew tired of the ceaseless fighting and signed a peace treaty. Both nations agreed to withdraw from Cambodia and to allow Ang Duong, a brother of the late king Ang Chan, to ascend the throne.

The treaty was supposed to restore neutrality to Cambodia. Ang Duong was crowned in 1848 in Phnom Penh, attended by representatives from both Thailand and Vietnam. The new king paid equal tribute to both neighbor nations, yet it is clear to historians that he wished to be rid of their interference. He encouraged the restoration of traditional Cambodian customs — for example, he forbade the use of Thai words for government functions and offices. He even sought outside help. The French, worried that Great Britain and the Netherlands had acquired extensive colonies and territories in Asia, had begun nosing around Southeast Asia, and King Ang Duong went so far as to send a letter to Napoleon III of France asking for his friendship and support. When a French representative offered to negotiate a full-scale treaty, however, Ang Duong refused. While he would have welcomed a show of strength from France to keep Thailand and Vietnam at arm's length, he was reluctant to give the French too much power over his ravaged country. "I have two masters already, who always have an eye fixed on what I am doing," he is said to have exclaimed bitterly to his councillors.

King Ang Duong died in 1860, after managing to hold Thailand and Vietnam at bay for more than a decade. This king, who is revered throughout Cambodia as a patriot and as the last king to rule without French interference, is the ancestor of Prince Sihanouk.

If the report is true that the Khmer army was several millions strong, it must have been by far the largest in the world of its day. But these peasants torn from their rice fields and forced into uniform fought with little enthusiasm and the wars dragged on until final defeat.
—NORMAN LEWIS
British writer, on the defeat of the Khmers by the Siamese in the 15th century

3

The Young King

King Ang Duong was followed on the throne by his oldest son, Norodom. The first few years of the new king's reign were uneasy ones, for he was confronted with renewed aggression from Vietnam, with religious and political rebellions in the northern provinces of his own kingdom, and with plots by three rival contenders for the throne, including one of his brothers. At the same time, through trade treaties and diplomatic efforts of various sorts, the French were gaining control over Vietnam. As they looked upstream toward Cambodia from their outposts along the southern part of the Mekong River, the French once again contemplated extending their influence into the troubled Cambodian kingdom.

From their headquarters in Saigon, Vietnam, French officials traveled upriver to Phnom Penh to call on King Norodom. Flattered by their gifts and their sympathetic attention, and intimidated by their gunboats and superior weapons, Norodom agreed to a proposal whereby he would make Cambodia a French protectorate — that is, he agreed to place Cambodia under France's protection against Thailand and other enemies, thus granting France some measure of domination over Cambodia.

The shy young man who came to the throne in April 1941 and was crowned in October seemed an unlikely candidate to dominate Cambodian politics for so many of the next forty years.
—DAVID CHANDLER
Australian scholar, in 1983

Sihanouk in 1941, at the funeral ceremonies for his uncle, King Sisowath Monivong. The French, then the colonial rulers of Cambodia, chose the 18-year-old Sihanouk to ascend to the throne.

The agreement that made Cambodia a protectorate was signed on August 11, 1863, by King Norodom and a French admiral. Hoping to hedge his bets, however, Norodom also signed a secret agreement with King Mongkut of Thailand, pledging his loyalty to Thailand in exchange for Thai recognition of his right to rule as king of Cambodia. When the French learned of this arrangement, they raised the French flag over Phnom Penh, claiming that Norodom had violated the terms of his agreement with them and had thus forfeited his kingship. Norodom, who had been on his way to Bangkok to take possession of the sacred Khmer coronation robes and emblems, scurried back to Phnom Penh and apologized to the French. From that moment, Cambodia belonged to France.

In the years that followed, France combined its administration of Cambodia with that of two other French protectorates in Southeast Asia, Vietnam and Laos. Together, the three countries were called French Indochina (the term Indochina is a reference to their geographic and cultural position midway between India and China). In 1867, the French managed to regain for Cambodia the provinces of Battambang and Siem Reap, which had been lost to Thailand.

King Norodom continued to sit on the throne of Cambodia, but only with French permission — and France controlled the country's foreign affairs and most of its internal affairs as well. The French tried to reform what they viewed as barbarous and wasteful customs; they were supported by Sisowath, Norodom's half brother, who was eager to occupy the throne and quite willing to cooperate with the French in order to do so. But Norodom stubbornly resisted the French efforts to change the Cambodian way of doing things, and he insisted on retaining as many of the remnants of royal power as he could. Finally, in 1884, the French threatened to depose him in favor of Sisowath. Under this pressure, Norodom signed a new treaty that changed Cambodia's protectorate status into that of a full-fledged colony, or possession, of France.

According to a contemporary, the french admiral in charge of southern Vietnam, "having no immediate war to fight, looked for a peaceful conquest, and began dreaming about Cambodia."

—DAVID CHANDLER
Australian scholar, quoting an 1885 account published in Paris (from his book *A History of Cambodia*, 1983)

The rural peasants of Cambodia had been down-trodden and exploited for centuries, but at this news they revolted in a wave of anti-French violence that rocked the country for two years. Although the peasant rebellion did not succeed in unseating the French, it was an ominous foretaste of things to come in the next century. At the time, however, the rebellion was soon forgotten, and the French continued to strengthen their control. In 1897, the French representative in Phnom Penh took control of the king's council of ministers. Norodom now lacked any real voice in Cambodia's government and was reduced to appearing in religious or ceremonial functions. He died in 1904, after 44 years on the throne, bitter and resentful over the way the French had seized control of his country.

Norodom's half brother Sisowath had waited a long time for the throne. He was in his sixties when he finally became king in 1904, and he ruled until 1927. King Sisowath's reign was a relatively peaceful era in Cambodian history. He cooperated fully with the French, and in turn they allowed him to retain the outward appearance of kingship so that the Cambodian people would believe that they were still being governed by one of their own. The only event of real political importance occurred in 1916,

A 1920 photo of the colonial palace in Saigon, Vietnam, from where the French ruled their possessions in Indochina: Cambodia, Vietnam, and Laos. The French took control of Cambodia in 1863.

Sihanouk's uncle, Monivong, who was named king by the French colonial authorities in 1927. Sihanouk was five years old at the time.

when peasants throughout the country rose up in rebellion against high taxes and forced labor on government projects. The rebellion ended peacefully when King Sisowath, the Royal Father, assured the people that he would take their problems under consideration.

Sisowath's throne was destined for his son Monivong, whom the French approved as a successor. Meanwhile, one of Sisowath's daughters, Kossamak Nearirath, had married a royal cousin named Norodom Suramarit. Their son Prince Samdech Preah Norodom Sihanouk Varman, was born on October 31, 1922. Five years later, old King Sisowath died, and Monivong, the uncle of young Prince Sihanouk, ascended the throne.

When Prince Sihanouk was a child, Cambodia was a French colony. During his lifetime, rapid and dramatic changes would propel Cambodia into independence and the modern world. During Sihanouk's childhood, however, life in Cambodia appeared to go on much as it had for centuries. Society was firmly divided into two main classes: workers and aristocrats. The workers were mostly peasant farmers, largely poor and uneducated. They numbered about 3 or 4 million. The aristocrats, numbering several thousand, were wealthy, well educated, and sophisticated. The middle class, consisting of government employees, merchants and shopkeepers, and students from the working class who had managed to obtain some schooling, was small and powerless—but growing.

Cambodia was an agricultural country with very little technology or industry. The majority of people lived in rural towns and villages. They had a strong commitment to religion and led traditional lives. On an average day, a peasant rose at sunrise to tend the paddies, as flooded rice fields are called. Each part of the year had its designated task: plowing, transferring shoots of rice into the paddies, or harvesting. The workday ended at sundown. There were few sources of entertainment, so family and village functions played an important role in the lives of rural folk. Much of rural life also revolved around the coming of the seasonal rains, the monsoons. The abundant rains were both a blessing and a source of worry for the farmer. Excessive rains might destroy the crops but compensate with a rich harvest of fish.

In the cities, the most coveted positions were civil service jobs in government offices. Educated young men concentrated all their efforts — and often a good portion of their families' wealth, in the form of bribes — on securing a position as a government worker or official.

Religion was common to city and village. The Buddhist *bonzes*, or monks, had substantial political power because of the deep-rooted religious beliefs of the people. Nearly all Cambodian boys of high social standing, including Prince Sihanouk, spent a year living and studying in a Buddhist monastery. Throughout his political life, Sihanouk recognized the power of the monks' endorsement. During his term as head of state, he participated each year in a religious rite in which he donned a robe of gold and a headdress that had belonged to his royal ancestors. Seizing a plow, he made the first furrow in the ground after the monsoon rains, thus beginning the planting season.

Cambodian Buddhist monks at prayer. Sihanouk grew up in a country where a large proportion of the population believed profoundly in Buddhism, and like many Cambodian boys of the era, he spent a year living in a Buddhist monastery.

The Royal Palace in Phnom Penh, built by the French for the Cambodian royal family. Sihanouk spent his early years there before being sent to Saigon and later to France for his education.

Although he was only one of many young princes in several lines of royal succession, Sihanouk's birth in 1922 was greeted with traditional celebrations, including offerings from his parents at many temples and gifts of food and coins to the people of Phnom Penh.

For the Cambodian people, the birth of a son or daughter traditionally calls for whatever celebration the family can afford. But it is also believed that the process of childbirth exposes the household to malignant spirits. The mother is expected to spend a few weeks in isolation. When she resumes her work in the house, she performs a rite in which she begs the forgiveness of the family members for exposing them to danger. This ritual is followed by a celebratory meal, and the whole family participates in the festivities.

When Cambodian boys and girls reach adolescence, they take part in a ritual called *kor sak*. A tuft of hair is cut off the top of the child's head to mark the passage of the child to the world of adults. At the same time, the neighborhood *achar*, or fortune-teller, predicts the child's fortune. But, although many traditional Cambodian customs applied to the royal family, Prince Sihanouk and his cousins had experiences quite unlike those of the typical Cambodian village child.

For one thing, they lived in palaces. The royal palace in Phnom Penh was built by the French for the Cambodian royal family soon after Cambodia became a protectorate. It was not a single building; rather, it was a large cluster or complex of palaces and related structures such as summerhouses and servants' quarters, all sealed away behind high walls. The buildings were all of one story only, as it was believed to be bad luck to stand above or below another person. Sihanouk's childhood home was built in the same grand style as the old palaces of Angkor, with massive stone portals and curling pagoda-style roofs, yet it was furnished with luxurious modern French furniture and household goods. There were huge grounds with beautiful gardens and intricate gateways leading from one part of the palace to the other. The palace compound was attended by a huge retinue of servants.

The princesses and princes were educated privately and later sent to finishing schools in France. Sihanouk, for example, was sent to a private school in Saigon, Vietnam, which was then the center of French culture in Indochina and is now called Ho Chi Minh City. When he was a little older, he at-

Sihanouk and his mother, Kossamak, are greeted by French president Vincent Auriol in 1949. Kossamak exerted a strong influence on the young prince; the selection of Sihanouk's brides was one of the tasks to which she zealously applied herself.

Sihanouk's second wife, Monique. Of mixed Italian and Cambodian ancestry, Monique wielded considerable personal clout in palace politics and, after Sihanouk's abdication in 1955, in government patronage.

tended school in Paris, France, and received some military training at Saumur, a town in western France that is the site of the French army's cavalry school and a training center for the French armed forces.

After the French took over, the kings and princes of Cambodia were able to lead rather leisurely lives. Many of them devoted their time to the patronage of art. They were wealthy and enjoyed an extravagant and colorful way of life. Many noblemen had more than one wife — a custom not uncommon in Cambodia until recent years. It was thought that the king, in particular, being more powerful than the ordinary man, could have more wives.

Princess Kossamak, Sihanouk's mother, was a strong influence on the young prince. It was said that she paid great attention to predictions made by astrologers and fortune-tellers about her son's life and kept him on a tight rein as a boy. She was in charge of his marriages and selected his brides. Sihanouk was first married to a princess named Suzanne. She was a quiet and reticent woman who after a few years retired from public life to become a Buddhist nun. She and Sihanouk had no children. His second marriage was to Monique, who was half European and half Cambodian. Monique was more outgoing than Suzanne had been; she enjoyed public appearances and took part in Sihanouk's activities as prince and later as king, frequently attending official functions with him. By the time of Sihanouk's abdication, she had become powerful and was considered to have reserved important positions in the government for her relatives.

Prince Sihanouk was only 18 years old when his uncle Monivong died in 1941. Monivong's death sparked a great deal of speculation and intrigue, for no one knew who the next king would be. Prince Monireth, Monivong's son, expected to ascend to the throne, but the real power to choose the new king lay with the French.

At this time, however, the French were having trouble of their own. For more than a decade, various groups in Vietnam had been rebelling against French rule; the most successful of these groups was the Indochinese Communist party, led by a radical named Ho Chi Minh. Furthermore, World War II was raging in Europe, embroiling France in yet another war with Germany, and now the Japanese were extending the war into Asia and the Pacific region. Before Monivong died, in fact, Japanese troops had marched into Phnom Penh and declared Cambodia occupied territory, but they allowed the French colonial administration to remain in charge.

Admiral Jean Decoux, the governor general of French Indochina, was faced with a difficult decision. He needed to appoint a new king quickly so that the Cambodian people would rally behind the royal family and not flock to the Communist banner being hoisted by Ho Chi Minh and his followers. Yet Decoux was worried about Prince Monireth; the prince had displayed signs of nationalistic feeling (that is, the belief that Cambodia should be self-governing), and Decoux feared that Monireth might lend his support to an independence movement. So Decoux settled on the young prince Sihanouk, a great-grandson of King Norodom, as the next king of Cambodia. He was certain that the French would more easily control Sihanouk than Monireth.

Sihanouk seemed an ideal candidate for the throne because his father was a Norodom and his mother a Sisowath; he thus united two rival factions within the royal family that had been competing for power since the death of King Norodom. In fact, the French justified their choice by claiming that they were actually restoring the throne to the original Norodom dynasty — after they had given it to Sisowath several generations earlier. Because he had studied in France and adopted French customs, Sihanouk did not seem in any way to be a political threat. The French expected him to be passive and to act as a buffer between the government and the local people. He was crowned on April 25, 1941, in Phnom Penh.

Many years later, Sihanouk told a group of diplomats, "The French chose me because they thought I was a little lamb. Later they were surprised to discover that I was a tiger." Indeed, it did not take long for the surprised French to discover that they had made the wrong choice. Sihanouk soon proved himself to be as fervent a nationalist as Monireth.

Sihanouk in 1941, wearing a black armband in mourning for his late uncle, King Monivong. "The French chose me because they thought I was a little lamb," said Sihanouk of the French colonial authorities' decision to install him on the throne. "Later they were surprised to discover I was a tiger."

4

War and Nationalism

King Sihanouk's opportunity to act upon his nationalistic beliefs came in March 1945, but the struggle for Cambodian independence can be said to have begun in 1940, when World War II was going against the Allies and the French were taking a beating at the hands of the Germans. Now the European colonies in Asia were targets for Japan's powerful army.

The Japanese army that was sent to Cambodia was heavily armed and outnumbered the French. Marching into Phnom Penh, the Japanese succeeded in taking over with few casualties. But instead of controlling all administrative functions, the Japanese government allowed the French administration to remain functional and assumed only military dominance.

The Cambodians, they have two faces, two aspects. They can smile, and they can kill.
—PRINCE NORODOM SIHANOUK

Sihanouk studies a map with a French military adviser in 1952, after the 29-year-old king took personal command of Cambodian troops fighting rebel forces. Though committed to gaining Cambodia's independence, Sihanouk needed France's support to consolidate his own power.

In the early 1940s Son Ngoc Thanh (shown here in 1972), a French-educated political scientist, led the movement to free Cambodia from France. Forced to flee to Tokyo during World War II, he returned in 1945 and eventually took over as prime minister after Sihanouk declared Cambodia independent.

The Japanese invasion was a turning point in the history of Cambodia, but only because it gave a focus to anti-French feelings that already existed within the population. France's domination of all aspects of Cambodian government had already given rise to feelings of dissatisfaction among Buddhist monks, who in 1942 staged a demonstration to protest the efforts of the French to romanize the Khmer language and to introduce the European, or Gregorian, calendar to replace the traditional lunar calendar.

The other dissatisfied faction within Cambodia consisted of students, chiefly young men who had studied abroad but who did not belong to the royal family. One of the leaders of this group was Son Ngoc Thanh, who had studied Western philosophy and political science and who returned to Cambodia to establish the first Khmer newspaper, called *Nagaravatta*. The newspaper was intended to remind the Cambodian people of their rich cultural heritage and to awaken nationalist sentiments. Thanh had the support of fellow students and of the religious community.

After landing in Indochina, the Japanese tried to make the French give Battambang and Siem Reap provinces back to Thailand. Son Ngoc Thanh led an organized demonstration of Buddhist monks outside the French embassy to protest this move. The protest started as a peaceful gathering, but it was not long before the crowd became excited and began throwing stones at the French embassy. The police intervened and dispersed the demonstrators. Thanh's two aides were arrested. In the confusion, Thanh was able to escape to Bangkok and finally to Tokyo. He spent the rest of the war years as a teacher in Tokyo.

The demonstration had been a protest against the French for allowing the Japanese to give away territorial rights. Thanh recognized the incident as an opportunity to turn the growing dissatisfaction among the people toward a nationalist cause. The French protectorate had demonstrated that it was unable to protect the rights of the Cambodian people; it was time, therefore, for the Cambodians to govern themselves. Thanh's followers in Phnom Penh continued to spread this kind of thinking.

In 1945, Japan began to suffer heavy casualties all over Asia. When it was certain that Japan was going to lose the war, France planned to resume its role as protector of Cambodia. The Japanese, however, disarmed all the French troops in Cambodia and gave their support to the independence movement in the countries of Indochina. On March 11, 1945, at the urging of the Japanese, Emperor Bao Dai of Vietnam declared the independence of his country from the French. On the following day, March 12, King Sihanouk proclaimed Cambodia independent. Son Ngoc Thanh was recalled from Japan and appointed foreign minister of the new country.

Independence was short lived. When the Japanese surrendered in August 1945, there was no Cambodian army to prevent the return of the French. Thanh was determined to keep the French out at all costs. He arrested all the other ministers, whom he feared might cooperate with the returning French, and he appointed himself Cambodia's first prime minister. He also revived his newspaper, the *Nagaravatta*.

Thanh's rise to power was so sudden that the wealthy and powerful nobles of Phnom Penh regarded him with suspicion and jealousy. It was known that Sihanouk did not approve of Thanh's methods. The king believed that the French could be made to leave Cambodia only through diplomatic means, so he dissociated himself from Thanh and denounced Thanh's actions publicly.

To counter the king's opposition, Thanh tried to strengthen his position by arranging a referendum, or vote by all the people. In September 1945, the referendum was held, and Thanh secured an overwhelming majority of the popular vote, suggesting that the people saw in him one who would lead the way to freedom. The royal family did not share this view. To the king and his fellow aristocrats, Thanh's victory was a threat to the privileges they enjoyed both as heirs to the monarchy and as rulers appointed by the French. Furthermore, Thanh was

Emperor Bao Dai of Vietnam, who near the end of World War II declared his nation independent of France with the help of Japan. The maneuver, also used by Sihanouk, was designed to hamper French efforts to resume control at war's end. But only two months after the end of the war, the French forced Bao Dai and Sihanouk to back down.

rumored to be associated with the Vietnamese Communists, whom the king opposed fiercely. The tension between Sihanouk and Thanh was so great that the king was threatened with arrest. Such a threat was nothing new to the king by now; throughout the war years, he had been treated more or less as a political prisoner under house arrest by the Japanese.

On September 11, 1945, a French officer parachuted into Phnom Penh without notice. This trespass undermined Thanh's authority and served as a reminder that the French were intent on regaining full control over Cambodia. Thanh's enemies within the country took advantage of this opportunity and sent one of Thanh's own cabinet members, Khim Tit, to Saigon to negotiate with the French for the prime minister's arrest. Meanwhile, King Sihanouk began to receive letters from French administrators in Vietnam. Three letters outlined France's proposition for Cambodia's future and asked Sihanouk to send a Khmer delegation to Vietnam to discuss the status of Cambodia with Admiral Thierry d'Argenlieu, the "High Commissioner of France." Sihanouk sent a firm reply that reminded the French of Cambodia's independent status under the Japanese occupation. He wrote, "We are disposed to deal with France and to have friendly relations with them of a political, economic and cultural order, relations that, at the same time, must not be of a nature to endanger the independence of our Country."

The French did not reply to this letter. To France, the "independence" of Cambodia had no legal foundation, having never even been acknowledged by the Japanese government in Tokyo. Plans for reinstating the French protectorate over Cambodia continued.

On October 8, Son Ngoc Thanh was arrested, taken to Saigon, and charged with treason for collaborating with the Japanese. He was sentenced to 20 years' hard labor. Due to his popularity, however, the sentence was waived, and he was kept under house arrest.

> *It is part of Cambodia's misfortune that it was always difficult for Western (and Soviet) officials to take Sihanouk seriously.*
>
> —WILLIAM SHAWCROSS
> American political
> historian,
> in 1979

King Sihanouk tried to distance himself as much as possible from the return of the French and the arrest of Thanh. He went on a religious pilgrimage on the day of Thanh's arrest. But he did sign a proclamation denouncing Thanh and reaffirming the loyalty of the Cambodian people to the French. Thanh's removal was an advantage to Sihanouk; it meant that when the French did leave Cambodia, there would be one fewer contender for power.

Once the Japanese had withdrawn from Indochina, French control was restored. But the pressure for change had been too great to be entirely ignored. Instead of returning to the status of a colony or even a protectorate, Cambodia was granted a constitution in 1947 and was made an associated state within the French Union in 1949. In theory, Cambodia was now permitted to govern itself. In matters of international, constitutional, or economic significance, however, the French commissioner had to give his approval. In spite of the changes that had taken place since the war, real power in Cambodia belonged to the Indochinese Federation, an administrative group that derived its power from the commissioner.

Cambodians bow to Sihanouk as a smiling Monique looks on. Beyond his divine status as a descendant of Vishnu, Sihanouk's charismatic charm, grace, wit, and often flashy behavior made him extremely popular among the people of Cambodia.

The return of the French proved to be disastrous for Thanh. After his arrest, his supporters fled to Thailand and to Thai-occupied areas of Cambodia. The Thai government allowed them to remain and often encouraged nationalist guerrilla movements. Thanh's supporters called themselves the Khmer Issarak, or Free Cambodians. After April 1947, when amnesty was extended to the nationalists, most of the Issaraks returned to Phnom Penh to join a new nationalist organization called the Democratic party, one of the first political parties to be formed under the constitution that made Cambodia a constitutional monarchy. Those Issaraks who remained in the jungle at this time were no more than roving bandits.

Thanh's exit from politics gave Sihanouk a chance to develop his own following. The king was a nationalist, too, but he believed that armed resistance was not the best way to achieve independence. He was convinced that the French could be made to withdraw only by legal and diplomatic means, and he intended to free his country without a war. In the meantime, he began to emerge as a distinctive personality, a flamboyant and charismatic ruler even in a time of pervasive change and upheaval.

Sihanouk was and is a multifaceted man. Early in his rule, he showed himself to be shrewd, ambitious, and often unconventional. He liked to mingle with the peasants and encouraged them to come to him personally. When he was first crowned, he tried to devote part of each day to private audiences in which he would listen to the problems of the common people; this custom had been practiced by the old Angkorean kings. Although Sihanouk did not directly change legal rulings in these cases, he was known to have paid for penalties from his own pocket and even to have commuted an execution sentence. Later, when his time was completely taken up with politics, he assigned subordinates to continue these audiences. Sihanouk's easy manner made him very popular with rural folk and humble people, who regarded him as a father figure.

Sihanouk also devoted some time and energy to the study of his country's history, and he formed

The common people of Cambodia have given us a magnificent example of farsightedness and genuine patriotism: they go along neither with the Khmer Rouge nor the outsiders [the Vietnamese]. They prefer to flee to Thailand, exposing themselves to the greatest dangers in the process, or else hide deep in Cambodia's forests, risking death from starvation, sickness, snakebite—or being eaten by tigers and wolves. That is what I call real courage and patriotism.
—PRINCE NORODOM SIHANOUK

distinctly personal opinions about it. In the 1930s and 1940s, most historians considered the decline of Cambodia to have come about during the Norodom and Sisowath dynasties, when the country fell under French control, but Sihanouk believed otherwise. He felt that the much-praised glory of the Khmer Empire and the Angkorean era was deceptive; instead, he thought that Cambodia's troubles had really started during the days of the Khmer Empire, with its multitude of invasions and political coups. Sihanouk sponsored the studies of a historian named George Coedes, who used the royal archives to demonstrate that Cambodia's instability could be traced to the mid-Angkor period. Sihanouk felt that it was shortsighted to blame all the country's problems on the Norodom and Sisowath dynasties. His view is generally shared to some extent by the most recent generation of scholars and historians.

Sihanouk show jumping in the early 1950s. Like many kings who ruled at the behest of colonial overlords, Sihanouk was known as a playboy and avid horseman, sports car driver, and musician.

A still photo from *The Apsara*, a 1966 movie written and directed by Sihanouk. Filmmaking was one of Sihanouk's hobbies, and though he starred in several of his own films, this one featured his daughter, Princess Buppha Devi, the dancer at center.

Like his historical theories, Sihanouk's behavior was often unconventional. He once invited diplomats from a number of foreign embassies in Phnom Penh to attend a "tree planting work-day." The invitation said that dress for the occasion would be work clothes, and the diplomats were taken aback to find that they were expected to spend a strenuous day laboring under the hot sun. They were rewarded for their efforts, however, with a sumptuous lunch.

The prince liked to give speeches spiced with wit and cutting comments. He was a passionate speaker who expressed his emotions freely. His messages were sometimes couched in metaphors or allusions that gave his listeners, including the diplomats and the foreign press, only a dim idea of what he was actually talking about. When he was annoyed, he did not hesitate to itemize the faults of the diplomats and his colleagues in speeches that were broadcast over the state-owned radio.

Both as prince and later as king, Sihanouk was known for his devotion to his hobbies: music, singing, racehorses, sports cars, and filmmaking. He

played the saxophone at parties. He wrote, directed, and starred in several movies. One of them, called *Shadow over Angkor*, featured Sihanouk and Monique as Cambodian patriots battling the United States Central Intelligence Agency (CIA). Another, called *The Apsara*, starred Sihanouk's daughter, Princess Norodom Buppha Devi, as a temple dancer. Sihanouk's films offer an insight into the prince's vision of Cambodia. They portrayed a romantic, glamorous, and mysterious land that bears little resemblance to the Cambodia of peasants and soldiers.

Sihanouk's movies were filled with mansions and sweeping avenues. He attempted to bring his ideal city to life in Sihanoukville, a seaport built with French aid. It was linked to Phnom Penh by the Cambodian-American Friendship Highway. The city was filled with parks and gardens, and a section was reserved for commercial and industrial uses. Today the city that was once called Sihanoukville is grimy, war torn, and in disarray; its new name is Kompong Som.

5

The King's Crusade

After World War II, France found itself unable to consolidate its hold over its former colonies in Indochina. In Vietnam in particular, the nationalist movement, led by the Communist guerrilla force called the Vietminh, had established a strong anti-French resistance. As much as the French tried to ignore and then suppress the nationalist movement in Vietnam, it grew rapidly until the Vietminh had gained the support of a significant percentage of the population. The French were able to establish control only over the southern half of the country; the north was taken over by Ho Chi Minh and the Vietminh, who proclaimed it the Democratic Republic of Vietnam in 1945. Almost immediately, the French invaded northern Vietnam, setting off an eight-year struggle with the Vietminh. These events were to have a profound effect on Cambodia.

I am the natural ruler of the country . . . and my authority has never been questioned.
—PRINCE NORODOM SIHANOUK
in 1953

In the post–World War II years, Sihanouk gained Cambodia's independence from France without resorting to warfare, then stepped down from the throne to lead his country into the world of modern politics.

Vietnamese Communist leader Ho Chi Minh led the guerrilla forces fighting for Vietnam's independence from France. By 1945, Ho's forces, the Vietminh, had established control over the northern half of the country. In the 1950s, the war between France and North Vietnam gradually spilled into Cambodia.

Under the leadership of Ho Chi Minh, the Vietminh adhered to the communist theories of Karl Marx. According to Marx, the economic system called capitalism, which is based on private ownership and enterprise, creates a select and elite group of individuals, the bourgeoisie, who eventually control a large portion of the nation's wealth. This inequality must give way to communism, an economic system under which there is supposed to be a fair distribution of wealth and no private ownership. Marx's followers believed that the change from capitalism to communism must involve an intermediate step, socialism, an economic system in which the means of production — land and industries — are owned by the people as a whole or by their representative, the state. Furthermore, say some versions of Marxist theory, because the bourgeoisie will not readily give up their property easily, the change from capitalism to socialism must be brought about by revolution.

The theories of V. I. Lenin, one of the first Communist leaders of the Soviet Union, seemed to Ho

Chi Minh and his followers to be even more applicable to conditions in Southeast Asia. Lenin argued that when Marxist concepts were applied to the local conditions and the historical background of a particular country, a unique new system would evolve. Hence, the form that revolution took in each country would depend upon the nature of political and economic oppression in that country. This meant that rather than attacking the economic system of colonialism as European Communists would do, Asian Communists would attack the political oppression of colonialism.

Along with resisting the French in Vietnam, the Vietminh began to encroach on Cambodian territory in the eastern regions. Some of Son Ngoc Thanh's followers, the Khmer Issarak, allied themselves with the Vietminh. This enabled the French to claim that the Vietminh and the Khmer Issarak were one and the same. In moving to crush the Vietminh, they could also strike a blow against the Cambodian nationalists.

In Phnom Penh, meanwhile, King Sihanouk was dealing with a new force in Cambodian history: party politics. Two parties emerged as the chief contenders for positions in the newly formed legislature, the National Assembly. One was the Liberal party, made up mostly of court officials, landowners, and aristocrats and headed by Prince Norindeth. The other was the Democrats, made up of teachers, students, and the Khmer Issarak. There was one important exception to the membership of the Democratic party, however — Prince Youtevong, a relative of Sihanouk, sided with the Democrats and would no doubt have emerged as the party's leader had he not died suddenly in 1947. Despite this setback, the Democrats won a large majority in the National Assembly and voted against the treaty that would make Cambodia an associated state within the French Union; according to the Democrats, the treaty left too much power in French hands. The king was displeased at this opposition to the course he wanted to follow, and in a display of the imperial power, he dismissed the National Assembly and signed the treaty in 1949.

Norodom, who is a man of thirty and looks twenty-one, is said by some of the French to be the most intelligent Cambodian.
—NORMAN LEWIS
British writer, who traveled through Cambodia in early 1950s, describing the king

King Sihanouk next assessed the situation in the frontier regions, where combined Issarak and Vietminh forces were harrying French troops. The king continued to maintain that the legal and diplomatic negotiation of a transfer of power would be the best policy for the country. Referring to Thanh's supporters, he said, "To support a band of pirates, as they would have had me do, to open our frontiers to the Vietnamese Vietminh, so that, in the name of a struggle against the French, they might massacre the little people, burn our bridges, our homes, our temples, our schools . . . was this a patriotic and acceptable solution for a King worthy of his name?"

After Prince Youtevong's death, the Democratic party failed repeatedly in its efforts to form a government. In 1949, a cabinet minister named Yem Sambaur formed a separate group within the party; he gained enough power to become prime minister. He became extremely unpopular with government officials, however, because he put pressure on the corrupt officials to stop the long-established practice of taking bribes. It was necessary for the king to intervene to allow Sambaur to retain his post.

Demonstrators in Cambodia show their opposition to the Vietminh in the early 1950s. Ho's forces used Cambodia and Laos as staging areas for operations in South Vietnam. King Sihanouk condemned the practice, thereby assuring himself of French support.

The problem of the Issaraks and the Vietminh refused to go away. Like many Cambodians, Sihanouk regarded the Vietminh with loathing, nationalists or not. The Vietnamese had been traditional enemies of the Cambodians for many centuries, and any alliance with them was regarded with suspicion. Sambaur and the king disagreed on this issue. The prime minister felt that the unyielding policies of the French would drive the Issaraks further toward the Vietminh. Sihanouk, fearful that both the French and the Vietnamese Communists were weakening the power of the Cambodian monarchy, disagreed. He maintained that if he could win the confidence of Chhoun Mochulpich, one of the most respected of the outlaw Issarak freedom fighters, half the battle would be won. Sihanouk issued an invitation to Chhoun, who was called Dap Chhoun (*dap* means "corporal"), to surrender and be forgiven for his crimes against the king.

Dap Chhoun, leader of Cambodia's anti-French guerrilla movement, surrenders his rifle to Sihanouk in 1949. In exchange, Sihanouk allowed Dap Chhoun and his rebel forces, which had been allied with the Vietminh, to join the royal army. The French, in turn, granted Cambodia limited autonomy.

In a dramatic and much-publicized ceremony, Chhoun came out of the jungle and laid his rifle at the feet of the king. He joined his Issarak band with the Cambodian army and was allowed to continue giving orders to his own men. The reconciliation between Sihanouk and Dap Chhoun was a triumph for the king. He had won over an important leader among the Issaraks and had also shown the French that he was in a position to negotiate with the guerrillas.

That same year, the Franco-Khmer treaty making Cambodia an associated state was signed. Sihanouk insisted on five major concessions from the French:

1. Genuine internal sovereignty for Cambodia.
2. Diplomatic relations with other nations and participation in the United Nations.
3. A rapid reduction of military zones and French presence in certain areas of Cambodia.
4. Pardon for the Issaraks.
5. Amnesty for all political prisoners, especially Son Ngoc Thanh.

As a result of this treaty, France recognized Cambodia as an independent country, except in judicial, military, and economic matters. Foreign policy had to be approved by the High Council of the French Union, which meant that every international agreement was subject to French policy and approval. After 1950, Cambodia was able to control its own foreign trade and finance, while customs and telecommunications were controlled by the board formed by the states of Indochina. In actuality, Cambodia was given control only over internal civilian issues; any contact with other nations had to be carried on through the French.

As part of the French Union, Cambodia received recognition from major Western powers. In Asia, however, only South Korea and Thailand showed any signs of support. Cambodia was admitted into international organizations, including the World Health Organization (WHO) and the United Nations Educational, Scientific, and Cultural Organization (UNESCO). This was the first step toward admission

> *Sihanouk resembled an old European monarch rather than the leader of a Third World country aspiring to a place in the modern world. He cherished the pastoral life and the arts while disdaining commerce, industry, and financial enterprise.*
> —ELIZABETH BECKER
> American journalist

into the United Nations. In 1951, Cambodia signed the Treaty of Peace with Japan. The French meanwhile evacuated troops from the provinces of Siem Reap and Kompong Thom in 1949 and from Battambang in 1951.

The results of the treaty were questioned by the Democrats, who felt that Cambodia's semi-independent status made a mockery of the struggle for independence. Sihanouk replied to this accusation by saying that he was "no longer a protected Sovereign but the Head of a legally free state." He was able to make the French agree to more settlements and to gain the worldwide recognition that he felt was a step toward total independence.

Cambodian ambassador to the United Nations, Nal Phleng, signs a peace treaty with Japan in 1951. Cambodia was not yet fully independent, but Sihanouk used its membership in the UN to press its case for total sovereignty.

Relations with the Democratic party further deteriorated when Prime Minister Yem Sambaur became the focus of a number of accusations. In January 1950, Ieu Koeus, who had served briefly as prime minister, was assassinated; many believed that Sambaur was behind the killing. Later, a strike by schoolchildren was broken up on Sambaur's orders. In the ensuing furor, the prime minister was forced to resign. The king took over the office of prime minister for a month before appointing his uncle Prince Monipong to the post. He governed without allowing the National Assembly to gather until 1951, when nine parties contested for the seats in the National Assembly. The Democrats won a majority of the seats, followed by the Liberals. Huy Kanthoul, a Democrat, was made prime minister.

The new government requested the return of Son Ngoc Thanh to Phnom Penh. Sihanouk's relationship with the Democrats had been uneasy, and this seemed a good opportunity to bridge the gap. He asked the French government to allow Thanh to leave Vietnam for Cambodia. The French agreed and arranged for Thanh's return.

More than 100,000 people greeted Thanh on his arrival. Cheering, they lined the streets from the airport at Pochentong into the city. Thanh had become the symbol of freedom and nationalism. He represented the uncompromising faction that demanded total independence. Having had no idea that Thanh's popularity was so great, Sihanouk was unpleasantly surprised. Such a show of welcome and honor had until then been given only to the king.

Thanh thanked Sihanouk for arranging his return. He had to be cautious in order not to irritate the king. Soon, however, he began publishing a paper called the *Khmer Krauk* (Cambodian Awakening). The paper had a strong anti-French slant and sparked an explosion of sentiment against the French. The paper was suspended in February 1952, and Thanh was in danger of being imprisoned again. The Democrats arranged for his escape, and he managed to flee to join the Issaraks along the Thai border.

Norodom Sihanouk is used to fighting against the odds. For nearly twenty years he rowed against the current of his country's past, and against foreign influence.

—GÉRARD BRISSÉ
French political historian,
in 1979

Sihanouk denounced Than[...] course, Thanh had accused the k[...] gullible, and an impediment to n[...] dependence. Sihanouk's detern[...] made it impossible for Thanh to [...] Penh. But his supporters rallied t[...] student demonstrations against th[...] in Phnom Penh — something that [...] heard of in centuries of Cambodian [...]

The Democratic party split into tw[...] that wanted to preserve the monarch[...] sympathized with Thanh. Thanh beg[...] cast clandestine radio announcements [...] ile. He accused the king of being a Fre[...] and said that Cambodia would be better [...] a monarch. In Phnom Penh, Yem Samba[...] pected of conspiring with Thanh. Ther[...] many complaints about Sambaur that P[...] ister Huy Kanthoul ordered his arrest.

In June 1952, Phnom Penh was a hotbed of confusion and political activity. Student demonstrations were complicated by the fact that French tanks patrolled the outskirts of the city. The Democratic government had no control over the situation, and the French made it clear that they would not listen to any demands. Sihanouk reviewed the situation and then dismissed the entire cabinet, assuming all the responsibilities and powers of the prime minister.

[...] tanks and armored personnel carriers move gingerly through flooded rice paddies in Vietnam in 1952. Unable to dislodge the expert guerrilla forces of the Vietminh, France's war to regain the Communist north was doomed to failure. The United States, meanwhile, began to aid French forces in an effort to forestall a Communist victory.

...uk informed the National Assembly that ...uld retain full powers for the next three years, ...t the assembly did not accept this decision. More demonstrations took place. In 1953, an ugly incident brought events to a stop. A bomb exploded in a French-run high school, killing a school official and a provincial governor. No one claimed responsibility. Once again, King Sihanouk dissolved the National Assembly and took control of the country. One of his first acts was to announce in a proclamation to the people that he would secure total independence for Cambodia within three years. He then appointed a National Consultative Council headed by his father to handle the day-to-day administration of the government. This left Sihanouk free to begin his fight for independence, a fight that he called the king's crusade.

He began the crusade by leaving Cambodia in January 1953 for a month's vacation in Italy. After traveling for a while, he finally established himself in a resort on the French Riviera. This action revived rumors about the "playboy prince," making it appear unlikely that anyone would take his freedom crusade seriously. In a time of extreme political crisis, his enemies pointed out, Sihanouk's first reaction was to establish a token government at home and travel for his own pleasure. Journalists and reporters had a field day listing his eccentricities and reporting his daily activities. The "Mad King of Cambodia" had become a media event.

But behind the facade of leisure, Sihanouk was beginning his fight for independence. He was accompanied by Prime Minister Penn Nouth and Sam Sary, his trusted adviser. He sent a message to the president of France, stating — in his own excessively eloquent rhetoric — the case for Cambodian independence. He admitted that the Issarak "say that I and my government are too Francophile to make our country really sovereign. Now, I ask you, Mr. President, what am I to reply to this propaganda when I am denied the means to fight effectively to defend my people . . . ? What am I to reply when the Issarak propaganda points out to the people and to the clergy that Cambodia is not really independent

since its king . . . has no power over the Frenchmen, Vietnamese, and the Chinese living in the country?"

The letter received no reply. Sihanouk wrote two additional letters emphasizing his demands. At that time, the French were in no position to deal with Cambodia; they were in enough trouble in Vietnam. The Vietnamese guerrillas had secured strategic positions, and the French army was barely keeping pace. President Vincent Auriol invited him to lunch, but there was no indication that there would be any change in the policy of the French in Cambodia. Later, when the king met with the French minister in charge of the Associated States, it was hinted that the crusade for independence might cost the king his throne. The French had given him the throne, after all, and they could just as easily take it away.

Sihanouk was furious at the threat. He decided that he would take his case to the international community, in the hope that the United States government would support the Cambodian cause and use its influence over the French. Letourneau heard of the king's plans to visit the United States and called the king's uncle, Prince Monireth, to get more information. After a three-hour conversation, he advised Monireth that it was advisable to caution the king against any unwise decisions. The message was clear.

Sihanouk in his limousine in Washington, D.C., in April 1953. His trip to the United States increased public awareness in the West of Cambodia's struggle for independence. However, the U.S. government, disappointed that Sihanouk could not promise to contain the spread of Communism, did not embrace the Cambodian king.

Sihanouk traveled to Ottawa, Canada, where he held a press conference. The Canadians were barely familiar with Cambodia; most of them knew little and cared less about the situation in Indochina. The king's next stop was New York City. From there he went to Washington, D.C., where he met with Secretary of State John Foster Dulles. The American agreed that the French had achieved very little in Indochina, but he was not convinced that the Indochinese states, if freed, would be able to stop the spread of communism from northern Vietnam. As a result, Dulles made no promises to the king, who was disappointed by this guarded attitude. Sihanouk returned to New York and arranged for extensive interviews with the press, resulting in front-page coverage in the *New York Times*. He left for Tokyo soon after.

In the meantime, the French invited a Cambodian delegation headed by Prime Minister Penn Nouth to come to Paris to reopen discussions. Sihanouk waited for the outcome of the talks in Tokyo. On May 9, 1953, proposals were signed by both sides. Sihanouk was asked to return to Phnom Penh to examine the results of the discussions. To his disappointment, the proposed changes were minimal.

Sihanouk returned to Phnom Penh with little to show for his efforts, but the public appreciated the king's devotion to the cause. Large crowds gathered to hear him proclaim the Crusade for Independence. There was a general feeling of unity and celebration. Issarak fighters came over to the side of the government and integrated their forces with the Cambodian army. In response to this, Sihanouk declared amnesty for the Issarak members who had surrendered.

His next move was a rather drastic step — one of many in a lifetime of political ups and downs. On June 12, he handed full powers to Penn Nouth and "exiled" himself to Thailand, vowing with as much publicity as he could muster not to return to his homeland until it was free. He had experienced gracious diplomatic treatment from the Thai government on an earlier visit, but this time the Thais were under pressure from the French not to treat the difficult Cambodian monarch especially well. So Sihanouk was housed in an ordinary hotel, and he was not granted an audience with the king of Thailand. With his dignity outraged, he left and took up quarters in Battambang Province in western Cambodia. Now he refused to return to the capital until his country was free.

In general, the foreign press sided with the French. One paper declared that "a country that has ten times as many monks as soldiers" had no chance against a Communist invasion. This news story had an unexpected effect; it united the Cambodians against the critical outside world, and they reaffirmed their support of the king. Four hundred men and women voluntarily took up military training.

French forces retreat after their defeat by the Vietminh at Dien Bien Phu in May 1954. The defeat signaled the end of French influence in Indochina; one year earlier, the French had granted Cambodia its independence.

The situation in Phnom Penh worsened. France had to send more troops to protect French citizens and property. In spite of — or perhaps because of — Sihanouk's bizarre international antics, the king's crusade for independence had become a full-fledged national movement that showed no sign of losing momentum.

Finally, not quite a century after they made Cambodia into a French protectorate, the French realized that their days in Cambodia were over. They offered to negotiate again, but the king demanded complete and unconditional independence. This time, the French listened. Full and complete independence for Cambodia was declared on November 9, 1953. The king returned to the capital in triumph. A new era in Cambodian history had begun. After 12 years of King Sihanouk's rule, and without a war with France, the country was independent for the first time in nearly 100 years.

Despite the victory for Cambodian nationalists, Indochina was a mess. The French and Vietnamese were still at war; one of the worst battles occurred at Dien Bien Phu, when the Vietminh seized a French garrison. The Vietminh were still disrupting life along Cambodia's borders as well. Laos, the third nation of French Indochina, was equally troubled. An international conference was held in Geneva, Switzerland, in May 1954 to resolve the problems of Indochina. (It was at this conference that Vietnam was formally divided into the two states of North Vietnam and South Vietnam.) The conference consisted of representatives from the three Indochinese states, France, the People's Republic of China, North Vietnam, the Soviet Union, the United States, and the United Kingdom.

Geneva was a triumph for King Sihanouk. The conference recognized his government as the only legitimate authority in Cambodia; this meant that neither the Vietminh nor their Khmer allies could get a foot in the door. The king's position was so strong that even Son Ngoc Thanh, his intractable enemy of more than a decade, appeared willing to cooperate with him.

Yet there remained those who criticized Sihanouk's policies or expected to share the power of government in the newly independent country. Sihanouk soon realized that although he had gained his country's freedom from France, he had not turned back the calendar to the era of absolute rule by the monarch. The political power of the future lay in the hands of party leaders, not of kings. Sihanouk saw this clearly, and he made another of the bold decisions that characterized his rule. In March 1955 he made his father king and stepped down from the throne. Now he was ready to compete for power in the modern arenas of the voting booth and the legislature — although he counted on his people's ancient reverence for their god-king to give him a boost at the polls.

The French delegation meets at the Geneva Conference on Indochina in July 1954. The conference recognized King Sihanouk's government as the sole governing authority in Cambodia.

6

The Fall from Power

The first few years of independence were difficult years for Cambodia. The conflict in Vietnam frequently surged across the border into Cambodia. In April 1954, just before the Geneva Conference, three battalions of Vietminh troops invaded Cambodia from Laos. A train traveling between Phnom Penh and Battambang was attacked, and about 100 Cambodians were killed. Troops were immediately sent to stop the invasion. The Cambodians secured a few initial victories, but their army was too ill equipped to force a total withdrawal of the Vietminh army. Sihanouk informed the United Nations of the invasion on April 23 and requested military protection from the United States. The Vietminh troops withdrew, but incursions into Cambodia by Communist guerrillas called the Vietcong, whose attacks on South Vietnam were supported by the government of North Vietnam, occurred with increasing frequency after the mid-1950s.

When one considers Sihanouk and his suggestions today, it is well to remember that in refugee camps in Thailand it is common to hear people say that they will never return to Cambodia under the Vietnamese nor under the Khmer Rouge, but only under Sihanouk. His was not a golden age, but it was the only age of peace.
—WILLIAM SHAWCROSS
U.S. political historian,
in 1984

Sihanouk in military uniform at independence day ceremonies in 1962. Throughout the 1960s Sihanouk maintained Cambodia's independence despite enormous military pressure from Communist North Vietnam and capitalist United States, which took over the war in Vietnam after France pulled out.

As a result of the Geneva Conference, France withdrew from Vietnam. But another important result of the conference was that it highlighted the schism between the Communist and anti-Communist nations that were represented. The Communist bloc, headed by the Soviet Union and the People's Republic of China (two nations that were not on the best of terms with each other, despite some basic similarities in political structure), not surprisingly favored the spread of communism throughout Southeast Asia. The anti-Communist bloc, headed by the United States, was firmly opposed to the spread of communism. The United States had been supplying the French government in Indochina with aid and made it clear that U.S. aid would be extended to the new anti-Communist regime in South Vietnam.

U.S. policymakers had decided that the strategic future of Southeast Asia could be explained in terms of what was called the domino theory. If the countries from the Chinese border to the foot of Southeast Asia were pictured as dominoes stacked one against the other, then the fall of one country to communism would result in the toppling of a neighboring country, and then another, just as the fall of the first domino in the row results in the eventual collapse of the whole row. The head of state of each nation in Southeast Asia was therefore expected to align his country with either the pro-Communist or the anti-Communist bloc.

Almost immediately, Sihanouk proved to be a source of frustration to American politicians whose view of Southeast Asia was shaped by the domino theory. Modeling his international strategy after that of India's prime minister, Jawaharlal Nehru, whom he had met and admired, Sihanouk declared that Cambodia was a neutral country. Not only did he show no interest in aligning with either bloc; he went so far as to say that Cambodia "had nothing against communist regimes as long as they do not interfere with Cambodia."

To Sihanouk, neutrality appeared to be his only hope of protecting Cambodia from aggression by either bloc and of keeping foreign nations from set-

Indian prime minister Jawaharlal Nehru greets Sihanouk in New Delhi in 1955. Nehru, whom Sihanouk greatly admired, was one of the founders of the nonaligned movement, in which the emerging nations of Asia and Africa declared their neutrality from the superpower struggle between the United States and the Soviet Union.

ting up military bases in the country (although at the Geneva Conference Sihanouk had reserved the right to ask for military aid for Cambodia from other nations, including the United States, if the Vietminh attacked Cambodia again). But to the United States, Sihanouk's embrace of neutrality was a rejection of U.S. goals for Southeast Asia. It meant that Cambodia would be open to Communist aid and might even become an ally of the Communists.

The conflict during and after the Geneva Conference between the non-Communist and Communist blocs for influence in Southeast Asia gave Sihanouk an insight into the future of his region. It strengthened his decision to follow Nehru's example and to be the leader of a neutral, or nonaligned, nation. He was encouraged to remain neutral by the the Chinese government, with whom he hoped to establish a trade and aid relationship; the Chinese, of course, were pleased that he did not align himself with the United States and hoped to exercise influence in Southeast Asia through a friendly relationship with Cambodia.

Indonesian president Sukarno (right) escorts Sihanouk and Monique past Indonesian troops during a state visit. Sukarno, another architect of the nonaligned movement, hosted the Bandung Conference in April 1955, where Sihanouk received assurances from China and North Vietnam that neither country would violate Cambodia's neutrality.

To further his position as the head of a neutral country, Prince Sihanouk led the Cambodian delegation to a conference of nonaligned nations at Bandung, Indonesia, in April 1955. Leaders of African and Asian nations — many of them newly created in the aftermath of World War II and the collapse of colonialism around the world — met to seek reassurance from the United States and the Soviet Union that these superpowers would not forcibly recruit nonaligned countries into the two blocs. In a speech to the assembled delegates, Sihanouk said that Cambodia would vigorously uphold what he called the Panch Shila, or Five Principles, that governed peaceful coexistence between neighboring countries; one of the principles prohibited any form of aggression against neighbors. This message, directed at the Communist nations of Asia, was not misunderstood. Later during the convention, Premier Zhou Enlai of the People's Republic of China and the North Vietnamese delegation met with Sihanouk over lunch and assured him that they too would follow the Panch Shila.

The prince did not want to cut off Cambodia entirely from possible benefits to be derived from the United States. In May 1955, he signed an agreement that allowed 30 American officers to study the Cambodian army and instruct Cambodian soldiers in the use of weapons. Although Sihanouk took special precautions to ensure that this agreement would not result in U.S. military base being built in his country, the Chinese press criticized him for signing it. As a neutral, however, Sihanouk felt free to deal with members of both blocs as he pleased.

With Cambodia established in the eyes of the world as an independent and neutral nation, Sihanouk's next task was to arrange for the national elections that had been agreed to at the Geneva Conference. Before scheduling elections, however, he wanted to make sure that the Democratic party would not threaten his own new party, the Sangkum Reastr Niyum. (The name of the party translates as People's Socialist Community, but the Sangkum did not promote socialist doctrines; its primary tenet was loyalty to Sihanouk as the liberator of Cambodia.)

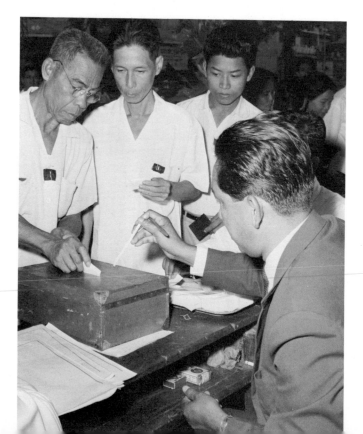

Cambodians cast their ballots in the nation's first-ever elections, held in September 1955. The constitution forbade the king from running for office, so Sihanouk, whose party controlled the media, stepped down and won the prime ministership overwhelmingly. He did not do well, however, among students and city dwellers.

It was a relief to Sihanouk to think that the political career of Son Ngoc Thanh, his old enemy, was over. Thanh had tried to reenter politics after his exile in the jungle. He sent a personal message to the king requesting a meeting. Sihanouk sent a harsh reply that said, "If the Monarch had not obtained the independence of Cambodia, the people would have condemned him and his entourage to death, for you and your men have denounced them as traitors."

The elections were held on September 11, 1955. The three parties that participated were the Sangkum, the Democrats, and a much smaller party called the Pracheachon, a group of Marxist Issaraks. The Democrats and the Pracheachon tried to undermine Sihanouk's support by suggesting that he had agreed to American aid — and therefore American domination — in place of French. The accusation became an issue that Sihanouk could not avoid, and he promised to bring up the question of foreign trade for the public to discuss.

The advantages in the election campaign clearly went to the prince's party, the Sangkum, which controlled the state-owned radio stations. The other two parties could not campaign as aggressively as they would have liked for fear of running afoul of the prince and possibly being prevented in some way from competing at all; the Pracheachon, in fact, had almost been refused permission to offer a candidate because the prince described it as "an international association." With power and popularity so strongly on Sihanouk's side, it surprised no one that the Sangkum swept to an impressive victory on voting day, winning 83 percent of the total vote. Sihanouk became the new prime minister, the head of Cambodia's government.

The election proved that the former king still had a powerful hold on the rural peasants who made up the bulk of Cambodia's population. The villagers voted for the familiar and revered figure of the man whom many of them still thought of as their god-king. They rushed to kiss the ground after he passed and treated his word as inflexible law. To such voters as these, Sihanouk's abdication and the formation of new political parties meant little.

> *He coveted and protected his unique position among the peasants as the anointed god-king. . . . Through public relations he convinced a large portion of the Cambodian population and much of the world that Cambodia was becoming a charming, neutralist paradise. . . . The prince enjoyed a status that would have been the envy of his immediate royal predecessors—total control over the country without the dominating protection of a foreign power.*
>
> —ELIZABETH BECKER
> American journalist, on
> Sihanouk in the 1960s

Among the educated monks, the students, and the city dwellers, however, the opposition parties did achieve some success — a fact that Sihanouk could not ignore. The prince recognized that from now on his authority and power would be under constant threat from these elements in Cambodian society. His country's newfound independence had brought with it the uncertainty and volatility of modern politics. Yet Sihanouk managed to remain the central figure in Cambodian politics and government for fully 15 years after the election of 1955. Throughout nearly all of that period, his control of the country was complete.

His first term as prime minister lasted for only three months. The Sangkum was a coalition, or association, of many groups that disagreed on several crucial issues; as a result, the party found it difficult to form a stable government in spite of the high degree of popular support it had received. There was constant argument in the National Assembly about the security of the country against invasion from the Vietnamese. Many Cambodians, including members of the Sangkum, were unconvinced that Sihanouk's neutral policy could prevent border wars. The dissension in the party became so uncontrolled that, in another of the grand gestures at which he had become an expert, Sihanouk resigned from his post as prime minister. As he had expected,

Sihanouk listens uncomfortably to U.S. secretary of state John Foster Dulles during Dulles's visit to Southeast Asia in 1955. The vehemently anti-Communist Dulles unsuccessfully pressured Sihanouk to join the pro-U.S. Southeast Asia Treaty Organization.

his resignation was followed by a series of mass demonstrations in his support at which crowds demanded his reappointment. With the populace growing angrier by the day, the Sangkum humbly looked to the prince to solve the problem. He did so by graciously resuming the prime ministership and retaining it on and off for a number of years.

During the first few years after 1955, Sihanouk's problems were mostly external ones. By the end of that year, he was being directly pressured by U.S. secretary of state John Foster Dulles to join the Southeast Asia Treaty Organization (SEATO). In spite of the Geneva Agreements, U.S. military buildup in Southeast Asia was expanding rapidly, but the United States was frustrated by Cambodia's rigid neutrality. The United States viewed SEATO as insurance against the spread of Communist wars in the region, and Cambodia was seen as the "missing link" in the series of allied countries from the Philippines to Thailand. Sihanouk, however, politely but firmly declined all invitations to join SEATO.

In January 1956, the prince visited a number of countries, including the U.S.-dominated Philippines. His neutral foreign policy was a source of concern to some of his neighbors. But Sihanouk remained convinced that if Cambodia stayed neutral, the threat of foreign aggression from both blocs would be lessened, and aid from both sides would help the country and its people. He further decided that a friendship with China would demonstrate to the Cambodian Marxists that he was not unsympathetic to their cause, although he would not directly support them. So he embarked upon a diplomatic visit to China.

The trip was a success as far as diplomatic protocol was concerned. Sihanouk had received a cool reception in the Philippines, but the Chinese government gave him the lavish and formal reception reserved for heads of state. Pleased by this, he signed the Sino-Cambodian Declaration of Friendship at the end of his visit — and in return was granted aid worth U.S. $22 million. Neutrality was paying off.

Sihanouk's course in foreign relations was shaped partly by his sensitive, even touchy, personality. He was upset by treatment that he felt was less formal or respectful than he deserved, and he was greatly put off by anything in the nature of brusque or assertive behavior on the part of American or European diplomats. As king in Cambodia, he had been accustomed to strict protocol and was acutely aware of the importance of his person. He assumed a paternal attitude toward his subjects, often making trips to distant villages in his helicopter and presenting gifts of cloth and utensils to the peasants. As prime minister, he continued to act and to be viewed as a father figure. But he never forgot diplomatic slights and retaliated with calculated rudeness when he could.

Sihanouk's relations with the United States were always tense, because he felt that the U.S. government was deliberately negligent about protocol. One incident with the American ambassador demonstrated Sihanouk's method of dealing with people he felt he had reason to dislike. When the ambassador arrived at Pochentong Airport, he was received by a junior protocol officer rather than a proper escort. When he tried to meet with Sihanouk, his appointment was postponed for three weeks. Finally, before the meeting, Sihanouk canceled the appointment abruptly to show his displeasure with the United States.

Chinese premier Zhou Enlai (left) is among those welcoming Sihanouk to Beijing in 1956. Sihanouk cultivated friendly relations with Communist China, the world's most populous nation and one of the strongest military powers in Asia. After this trip, China sent $22 million in aid to Cambodia.

Anti-American protesters stone the U.S. embassy in Phnom Penh in 1964 as government police offer only token resistance. With the United States becoming increasingly involved in the war in Vietnam and further pressuring Cambodia to abandon its neutrality, relations between Phnom Penh and Washington became more strained as the 1960s wore on.

Relations between the two countries grew steadily worse during the early 1960s. In 1963, Sihanouk ordered the U.S. Aid for International Development mission to leave the country; a year later, a stone-throwing mob, probably supported by the Cambodian government, attacked the U.S. embassy in Phnom Penh. In May 1965, Cambodia formally broke off diplomatic relations with the United States, ordering the ambassador and his aides to leave the country. Yet Sihanouk was capable of whimsical good nature as well as peevishness and sternness. On one occasion in 1968, when some American soldiers who were supposed to be landing a barge in Vietnam got lost and wandered into neutral Cambodia, Sihanouk angrily threw them in jail and lodged a stiff protest with the United States; almost immediately, however, he sent his personal tailor to the jail to make new white linen suits for the American prisoners so that they could join him on the official reviewing stand at Cambodia's independence day parade, and after the parade he treated them to an expensive meal at Phnom Penh's finest restaurant and let them go.

Sihanouk also felt slighted by the United Nations over matters of protocol. When he attended the 15th session of the United Nations General Assembly in New York City in 1960, only one security officer was assigned to him, while some other heads of state had large security retinues. Offended by this inconsistency, Sihanouk dismissed the security officer, only to be stopped on his way into the UN chambers because no one knew who he was and he was not accompanied by a security officer. One incident in particular especially angered Sihanouk: While he was being driven to the United Nations building, his car was pulled over to make way for the motorcade of Nikita Khrushchev, the Soviet premier.

The British got into Sihanouk's bad books when Prime Minister Harold Macmillan invited the prince to visit Great Britain. After Sihanouk accepted, Macmillan declared that the visit would be an unofficial one, not a state visit. Piqued, Sihanouk declined the offer and instead accepted invitations to make state visits to the Communist countries of Czechoslovakia, Mongolia, and China. Macmillan then wrote to the prince to inform him that the visit could be made an official one if he wished, but the damage had been done, and Sihanouk declined once again.

Sihanouk listed and never forgot such incidents, which he felt were insults to Cambodia as well as personal slights. He recognized that Cambodia was a small country and that his role in world politics was measured by the size of the country. Furthermore, he knew that his uncompromisingly neutral stance put him in an unfavorable position with the leaders of anti-Communist nations. Nevertheless, he continued to insist upon recognition and respect from other world leaders.

Over the years, Prince Sihanouk held a variety of titles: Among them were prime minister, foreign minister, and United Nations representative. When his father, King Norodom Suramarit, died in 1960, no one succeeded to the throne, which no longer wielded any power at all. Instead, Sihanouk had himself proclaimed formal head of state — the role that had been filled by the king — as well as head of government. Cambodia's ancient monarchy had ended.

Sihanouk addresses the United Nations in New York in 1960. Sihanouk felt slighted by the rudimentary security the UN arranged for him, particularly when his limousine was pulled over on a New York street to allow Soviet premier Nikita Khrushchev's motorcade to pass.

By the mid-1960s, despite the international juggling act by which the prince maintained Cambodia's neutrality and wooed large sums in foreign aid into his country, all was not well in Cambodia. The United States and South Vietnam were now fighting North Vietnam just across the border. After 1965, when he broke off relations with the United States, Sihanouk began to align Cambodia more closely with China and North Vietnam. Because he believed that the Communists would eventually control all of Vietnam, he felt it was important not to make enemies of them. Therefore, when the army of North Vietnam and the Vietcong guerrillas began crossing the border to set up secret military bases in the jungles of Cambodia, he did not protest; furthermore, he allowed the North Vietnamese to use the port of Sihanoukville to supply these bases. In a desperate attempt to preserve ties with both sides, he also secretly told the United States that he would not protest if it decided to bomb the Vietcong hideouts in Cambodia. When these bombings began in 1969, killing and injuring Cambodian civilians along with the Vietcong, many Cambodians felt that their leader and former king had betrayed them.

Part of the eight-day funeral ceremonies for King Suramarit in April 1960; here Queen Kossamak lights the cremation fire that will reduce her husband's body to ashes. With the death of Sihanouk's father, the centuries-old institution of the Cambodian monarchy came to an end.

A U.S. Marine patrol in South Vietnam in 1965. By that year the Americans had joined the conflict and escalated it into a full-scale war. The Americans and their U.S.-backed military regime in South Vietnam fought against the North Vietnamese and the Communist Vietcong guerrillas.

As the 1960s drew on, Sihanouk grew highly unpopular with several elements in Cambodian society. He had tried to steer a middle-of-the-road course in domestic affairs, not allowing any one faction to rival him. But now he was under attack from both ends of the political spectrum. On the right were conservative and reactionary Cambodians — supported to some extent by the United States — who felt that Sihanouk was too friendly with the Communists and wanted Cambodia to pursue an anti-Communist course. The leaders of this faction were General Lon Nol and Prince Sisowath Sirik Matak, a relative of Sihanouk. These two found an ally in Son Ngoc Thanh, who was the leader of an anti-Sihanouk group called the Khmer Serei. On the left were liberal and radical Cambodians — most of them young people who had been educated abroad — who wanted a freer, more open political atmosphere and resented the fact that Sihanouk crushed all dissent. This leftist faction, which promoted Communist doctrines, organized itself into the Khmer People's party but was more often called the Khmer Rouge (*rouge* is French for "red," and red is the color associated with international Communism). The Khmer Rouge gradually gained a following in rural Cambodia. Among its leaders were a handful of Paris-educated leftists, including Son Sen, Ieng Sary, and Saloth Sar, who were to play significant roles in Cambodia's future.

Several attempts to overthrow or assassinate Sihanouk were made during the mid-1960s. One involved Dap Chhoun, the former freedom fighter, and Sam Sary, a onetime close associate of the prince. On another occasion, a mysterious present was sent to Sihanouk's mother, who was known to enjoy opening her own mail. The package contained a bomb, but the explosion killed only a secretary and an attendant. Sihanouk believes that these and other threatening incidents were organized or supported by the United States's CIA. Although the extent of CIA involvement in Southeast Asian affairs has never been made fully clear, many political historians agree that the CIA was at least aware of the attacks on Sihanouk and hoped that he could be removed from power.

Sihanouk's most dangerous political rival turned out to be General Lon Nol, whom he had grown to trust. Sihanouk later recalled, "As for Lon Nol, I had entrusted him with the post of Commander-in-Chief of our armed forces. . . . Lon Nol was responsible for national security."

The crisis that led to Sihanouk's downfall began with the sixth National Assembly election in 1966. Over the years, Sihanouk had relaxed his control over the elections, and now he allowed candidates whom he had neither appointed nor approved to run for election. Lon Nol and his backers mounted an expensive campaign — possibly funded in part by the United States — to win votes, giving gifts to voters and toys to their children across the country. As a result, Lon Nol's party triumphed at the polls, and Lon Nol became prime minister. Sihanouk remained powerful, however, and now he associated more closely with leftists in the capital, among them Khieu Samphan. Like the Khmer Rouge leaders, Samphan was destined to figure in Cambodian history.

You met corruption at every stage of life. . . . You could bribe your way through the courts—you could bribe your way through anything. The only people you didn't bribe were the monks: you just gave them money instead.

—SOMETH MAY
Cambodian refugee,
describing life in
Sihanouk's Cambodia
in the 1960s

The new prime minister made a serious mistake in 1967. He ordered his troops into the fertile Battambang region and began to evict the villagers, claiming that they did not hold legal title to the land. According to Cambodian tradition, the people who cultivate the land automatically own it, so the eviction was a violation of custom. The people of Battambang, among whom were many of Chinese and Vietnamese descent, protested violently. The protest rapidly escalated into a peasant rebellion. Lon Nol blamed it on the Chinese and Vietnamese villagers and on the Khmer Rouge. Sihanouk also placed the blame for the uprising upon the Khmer Rouge and other leftist groups. In a sudden reversal of policy, he ordered a police crackdown on leftists in the capital, forcing Khieu Samphan and others to flee to the countryside to join the Khmer Rouge. But the anger of the populace against Lon Nol was such that he resigned for a time, resuming office in 1969.

A B-52 bombs Cambodia during secret U.S. air raids against the neutral nation in 1969. U.S. Air Force bombing runs in North Vietnam, by far the largest in history, were expanded into Cambodia, ostensibly to destroy Vietcong supply lines. The raids failed, killing hundreds of civilians and bringing the war directly into Cambodia for the first time.

By that time, the crisis in Cambodia was coming to a head. Now alarmed at the growing scale of North Vietnamese and Vietcong military action in his country, Sihanouk called for a withdrawal of all Vietnamese troops from Cambodian soil. The conservatives who supported Lon Nol and Sirik Matak continued to demand a Vietnamese withdrawal, but Sihanouk's diplomatic efforts failed to dislodge the Vietnamese. The conservative faction loudly blamed Sihanouk for letting the Vietnamese enter the country in the first place, and an ever-larger segment of the population shared this view. Sihanouk's popularity fell to an all-time low. In January 1970, he left the government in the hands of Lon Nol and went to France for his annual vacation and health treatment, planning to return by way of Moscow and Beijing, China.

A French general decorates Lon Nol, then Cambodia's armed forces minister, in 1956. In 1966, as a staunchly anti-Communist general and commander of Cambodia's armed forces, he was elected prime minister — in large part because the U.S. government made huge donations to his campaign.

No sooner had the prince left Cambodia than Lon Nol ordered Vietnamese Communist forces to evacuate the country. They refused. Anti-Vietnamese riots, perhaps instigated by Lon Nol's supporters, broke out in Phnom Penh and across the country. Angry mobs sacked the embassies of North Vietnam and South Vietnam. On March 18, claiming that Sihanouk had proven himself unable to deal with the Vietnamese crisis, Lon Nol arranged a coup in which the National Assembly declared the prince deposed as head of state and gave full power to Prime Minister Lon Nol. The first act of the new head of state was to order the international airport guarded so that the prince would be unable to reenter the country if he tried to return.

In the meantime, Sihanouk had left France for the Soviet Union. He was informed of the coup by Soviet premier Aleksey Kosygin as he prepared to board a flight to Beijing.

Overturned trucks burn in the aftermath of rioting against Vietnamese in Phnom Penh in 1970. The rioting grew out of demonstrations, backed by the Cambodian government, against the presence of North Vietnamese and Vietcong troops on Cambodian soil. Sihanouk, in France at the time, was blamed for the problems with Vietnamese forces and was overthrown as head of state.

7

Riding the Tiger

Shocked and enraged by the coup that had taken place during his absence, Sihanouk continued on to Beijing as planned. Although he had voluntarily given up more than one powerful post during his career, he had not been prepared to be thrown out of office — and out of his country. He intended to fight back, hoping to rally international opinion against Lon Nol.

The Chinese invited the prince to take up residence in Beijing. There he set up a government-in-exile that he called the Royal Government of the National Union of Cambodia. This government was granted diplomatic recognition by the heads of state of China, North Vietnam, and South Vietnam. The United States, on the other hand, openly backed the Lon Nol regime and immediately granted it $10 million in aid. Emory Swank was appointed the new U.S. ambassador to Cambodia; he was the first to serve there since 1965.

In Cambodia, Sihanouk was immensely popular. We barely noticed his faults, like allowing corruption to go unpunished, and keeping incompetent people in the government. Few of us were educated enough to care. When he spoke to us in his loud, high-pitched voice, shouting and gesturing wildly, eyes bulging with excitement, we listened with respect.
—HAING NGOR
Cambodian refugee

A soldier of Lon Nol's U.S.-backed Cambodian government leads a blindfolded Khmer Rouge guerrilla to an interrogation session in 1973. The Communist Khmer Rouge won the civil war and unleashed one of the most murderous regimes of the 20th century.

Lon Nol leads a contingent of officers in a parade in Phnom Penh. Having forced Sihanouk into exile, the general built up his army with huge amounts of American military aid.

In addition to his government-in-exile, Sihanouk also headed a semimilitary organization called the National United Front of Cambodia (NUFC), which was dedicated to overthrowing Lon Nol's government. In radio broadcasts from Beijing, transmitted through Hanoi, North Vietnam, into Cambodia, he denounced his former general as a traitor. He appealed to the intellectuals and the staunch patriots of the country to resist the Lon Nol government. These broadcasts won some support. Three members of the National Assembly who had long opposed the prince promised to support him unconditionally against Lon Nol. In addition, the rural public gathered in large demonstrations in the countryside, carrying banners and portraits of the prince and brandishing farm tools as weapons.

Lon Nol reacted by claiming that the demonstrations were organized by the Vietnamese. His troops massacred large numbers of villagers. On April 13, 1970, 500 Vietnamese Catholics who were citizens of Cambodia were killed in Phnom Penh. Military actions failed to halt the demonstrations, however.

The situation grew so bad that Sihanouk advised from Beijing against the armed struggle of the people so that the killings would stop. Large numbers of Lon Nol's own troops deserted and joined resistance groups because they could no longer overlook the fact that they were being ordered to slaughter their own people.

Cambodian political life was turbulent and factional under Lon Nol. He and his followers held a trial at which Prince Sihanouk and Princess Monique were sentenced to death for crimes against the state; of course, it was not possible to carry out the sentence. Son Ngoc Thanh's fate was just the opposite. After years of shadowy semiexile in the border jungles, he and his Khmer Serei, who had cooperated with Lon Nol, were invited to return to Phnom Penh.

In October 1970, Lon Nol formally abolished the Cambodian monarchy and renamed the country the Khmer Republic. From the start, however, his control was shaky. Even with U.S. support — which ended in August 1973 (when the United States stopped bombing the Cambodian countryside)—he was unable to keep the Vietnamese Communists from operating within Cambodia and attacking his army. Side by side with these Vietnamese Communists fought the Khmer Rouge, the Cambodian Communist movement, which firmly opposed Lon Nol. Over the next few years, the Khmer Rouge gained numbers, strength, and skilled leadership.

Some of the 500 victims of the April 1970 massacre of Vietnamese Catholics in Cambodia float down the Mekong near Neak Leung; all the victims were ethnic Vietnamese, but citizens of Cambodia. The massacre was instigated by the Lon Nol government and took advantage of age-old hatred between the Khmer and Vietnamese peoples.

By 1973, Lon Nol was forced to admit that the Cambodian rebels posed a greater threat to him than Vietnam did.

Sihanouk's relationship with the Khmer Rouge changed after the coup. Although he had wavered in his position toward Cambodian leftists, sometimes leaning in their direction and sometimes repressing them, after 1970 he allied himself with the Khmer Rouge. He felt that he and the Communists shared a common enemy in Lon Nol and should work together to overthrow him. To many Cambodians and others around the world, the exiled prince served as a symbol of legitimate government for Cambodia — and this was an image that Sihanouk did his best to encourage. But the emergence of effective leaders among the Khmer Rouge in the early 1970s led to a decline in the prince's importance. Although he spoke out in favor of the goals and activities of the Khmer Rouge, Sihanouk actually had very little to do with their long-range planning or the day-to-day conduct of the guerrilla war against Lon Nol.

Wearing a garland of flowers, Son Ngoc Thanh, Sihanouk's longtime opponent, arrives in Saigon in 1972. After years as an anti-Sihanouk rebel in the jungles, Lon Nol brought him into the government to serve as prime minister.

American antiwar activists demonstrate in Washington, D.C., in 1969. Domestic opposition to U.S. involvement in the war in Southeast Asia began in 1965 and grew, forcing the start of a gradual U.S. withdrawal from the war in 1969. In 1973 the antiwar movement helped force the U.S. government to halt the bombing of Cambodia.

Chief among the Khmer Rouge leaders were Khieu Samphan, Ieng Sary, and Saloth Sar, who had changed his name to Pol Pot. These men accused Sihanouk of having mismanaged the government while it was under his control. They showed themselves increasingly independent of the prince, so that by 1973 he admitted that he had lost control of the revolutionary movement, even though he was its official head. In terms of his relationship with the revolutionaries, Prince Sihanouk found himself in the position of a man riding a tiger — in trouble if he tries to get off and in trouble if he stays on. Having allied himself with the Khmer Rouge, he could not very well disavow them; such an act would mean that he would be entirely shut out of events in Cambodia. But he realized that the goals of the Khmer Rouge were not the same as his, and it became increasingly apparent that the revolutionaries were uncertain allies with whom it might prove difficult or dangerous to collaborate.

Khmer Rouge leader Ieng Sary accompanies Sihanouk and Monique to a jungle base in northwestern Cambodia in 1973. Sihanouk allied himself with the Khmer Rouge, who were slowly but surely defeating the forces of the Lon Nol government.

By the time the United States ended its bombing of guerrilla bases in August 1973, the Khmer Rouge controlled nearly 60 percent of Cambodia, including all the major routes into Phnom Penh. It was estimated that at least a quarter of all Cambodians either belonged to or sympathized with the Khmer Rouge.

Events moved swiftly from that point. Khmer Rouge forces surrounded Phnom Penh, which was swollen by the flood of refugees — perhaps as many as 2 million of them — from the ravaged and war-torn countryside. On New Year's Day, 1975, the Khmer Rouge launched an all-out attack against the capital, cutting it off from the outside world. After several months of rocket barrages and constant heavy fighting, Phnom Penh surrendered on April 17. The U.S. mission and Western diplomats fled the fallen city a few steps ahead of the advancing peasant army, as did Lon Nol, who managed to escape to Hawaii.

The Cambodian people who had hoped that a Khmer Rouge victory would bring peace were in for a grim surprise. The Khmer Rouge leaders immediately embarked upon a massive and disruptive scheme to rebuild Cambodian society. This plan was to result in four years of violence and death.

The residents of Phnom Penh and all other cities were marched at gunpoint into the countryside, where they were housed in labor camps and ordered to farm the land. Thousands of people died during the evacuations and forced marches. Because the new regime celebrated peasants and scorned intellectuals and those with pro-Western leanings, thousands more were killed simply because they were doctors or teachers or could speak English or French. Anyone who was connected in any way, however innocent, with the Lon Nol regime was executed.

Sihanouk returned to Phnom Penh in September and was made formal head of state. He set out on an 11-nation tour to win international support for the Khmer Rouge. But the uneasiness he had felt about throwing in his lot with the revolutionaries had been justified. Now that they were in control, Sihanouk soon discovered, the Khmer Rouge did not need a prince. In January 1976, the Khmer Rouge introduced a new constitution and renamed the country Democratic Kampuchea (D.K.). Three months later, Sihanouk resigned as head of state — possibly under threat — and was placed under house

U.S. ambassador to Cambodia John Guenther Dean carries the American flag as he and embassy staff arrive in Thailand after fleeing Phnom Penh in April 1975. A few days later the Americans also fled South Vietnam, signaling the defeat of the United States in Southeast Asia.

A worker in post—Pol Pot Cambodia cleans a human skull, one of hundreds of thousands exhumed from the fields where the Khmer Rouge carried out mass executions. Human remains were still being uncovered throughout Cambodia more than a decade after the Khmer Rouge were driven from power.

arrest with his family. What he had expected to be a triumphant return to his homeland had turned into a nightmare. In the years that followed, he remained a virtual prisoner of the Khmer Rouge. Although his own safety and that of Princess Monique does not appear to have been threatened, at least five members of his immediate family and other members of the royal family were taken from their homes and were never seen again.

Meanwhile, the Khmer Rouge had set up a new government. In April, Pol Pot was named premier of Democratic Kampuchea and Khieu Samphan became head of state. The following year, the Communist party of Kampuchea was declared to be the country's governing body; the National Assembly had long since vanished.

Pol Pot's regime is now regarded as one of the

cruelest in modern history. The ruling party dealt severely with anyone who was believed to pose a threat or to voice a criticism; mass arrests and public executions were common. Khmer Rouge officers, many of them peasant children, were given weapons and authority, and killing sprees were frequent. Cambodian Muslims, Catholics, and people of Vietnamese descent were persecuted with special rigor. Families were separated; religion was suppressed, and monks were killed or forced into field labor; and schools, money, and postal services were eliminated. Thousands of Cambodians tried to escape to Thailand. Many died in the attempt, but those who survived began to tell the outside world what was going on inside Democratic Kampuchea. Pol Pot's brutality was condemned by the international community, but he persisted in his genocidal course.

As so often in the past, Vietnam interfered with the direction of Cambodian history. As relations between the Soviet Union and China deteriorated, Vietnam, which was backed by the Soviets, grew increasingly hostile to Cambodia, which was backed by China. At China's urging, Cambodia attacked Vietnam, and the Vietnamese retaliated. By the middle of 1978, the two nations — both of whose economies had been ravaged by earlier wars — were engaged in full-scale combat. A D.K. officer named Heng Samrin defected to Vietnam, where the Vietnamese named him head of a new Cambodian government. On December 25, 1978, Vietnam invaded Cambodia in full force, hoping to topple the government of Democratic Kampuchea and place Samrin in power.

A rare photo of Pol Pot, leader of the Khmer Rouge. After the guerrillas' victory, Pol Pot became premier of Democratic Kampuchea, as the Khmer Rouge renamed Cambodia. The Pol Pot regime immediately began the forced removals and mass killings that transformed Cambodia into a vast concentration camp.

The Vietnamese army, which was much larger than that of Democratic Kampuchea, captured Phnom Penh on January 7, 1979. The Khmer Rouge and D.K. forces, with Pol Pot among them, fled to the hideouts in the mountains and jungles of the frontier provinces from which they had emerged victorious a few years before. Several hundred thousand desperate Cambodians, too, fled toward Thailand to escape the invading Vietnamese. The regime of Democratic Kampuchea was over, but no one knew what might happen next.

It is still not known for certain how many Cambodians perished in the prisons, torture centers, and labor camps of Pol Pot. Estimates vary from slightly more than 1 million to as many as 2.5 or 3 million victims — out of a total population that had numbered little more than 7 million in 1975. What is known is that the regime of Democratic Kampuchea was marked by cruelty, irrationality, and murder on an almost unprecedented scale. The world is still learning about what happened in Cambodia between 1975 and 1979 from tales told by survivors of the holocaust.

The victorious Khmer Rouge guerrillas, many of them teenagers, rounded up and shot intellectuals, doctors, Buddhist monks, Muslims, Catholics, and people of Vietnamese descent; much of the rest of the population was made to work from dawn to dusk on large collective farms.

8

The Freedom Fighter

Freed from three years of house arrest by Pol Pot on the day before the Vietnamese army marched into Phnom Penh, Prince Sihanouk once again fled to Beijing. He was not the only Cambodian leader to seek asylum in China. Khieu Samphan arrived there at about the same time as the prince, and Pol Pot showed up later. The prince and the fallen heads of the Khmer Rouge were united in denouncing Vietnam as an aggressor. Sihanouk, however, also denounced Pol Pot, Khieu Samphan, and the Khmer Rouge for the atrocities of Democratic Kampuchea. China, meanwhile, was happy to play host to all parties, hoping to wield influence in Cambodia in the future no matter which faction was restored to power. China did attempt to drive the Vietnamese from Cambodia by force with a small invasion in late 1979, but this attempt failed, and the Chinese were resigned to regaining their influence through diplomatic means and through gifts of guns and money to the anti-Vietnamese guerrillas.

I am not a member of the Khmer Rouge team. They are courageous fighters for . . . I cannot say freedom, but for national independence and territorial integrity.
—PRINCE NORODOM SIHANOUK
after being released from
house arrest in 1979

Sihanouk, accompanied by Khmer Rouge soldiers, tours a refugee camp in Thailand in 1983. Although he condemned the murderous Pol Pot regime that ruled Cambodia, Sihanouk was forced to ally with them after Vietnamese forces invaded the country and drove the Khmer Rouge out in 1979.

Chinese leader Deng Xiao-
ping with Sihanouk in 1985.
China harbored the exiled
prince and supported him in
his efforts to oust the Vietnamese from Cambodia.

In Phnom Penh, Heng Samrin was appointed
party secretary, and Hun Sen was made prime minister of Cambodia's new regime, which was called
the People's Republic of Kampuchea (PRK). The war
with Vietnam was officially over, but for some years
Vietnam continued to exercise tight control over the
PRK regime, which amounted to nothing more than
a puppet government whose strings were pulled in
Vietnam — which in turn was influenced by the Soviet Union. Only Vietnam, the Soviet Union, and a
handful of Soviet allies granted diplomatic recognition to the PRK.

Diplomatically, in fact, Cambodia's status remained confusing throughout the 1980s. Only the
Soviet-aligned nations and India regarded the PRK
as the legal government of Cambodia. The United
Nations refused to recognize the PRK because that
would imply that the UN was willing to overlook
Vietnam's blatant invasion of Cambodia. As a result
— and despite the abhorrence felt by the world for
Pol Pot's regime — Democratic Kampuchea has continued to occupy Cambodia's official seat in the
United Nations. Ieng Sary, one of Pol Pot's lieuten-
ants, has spoken frequently at UN sessions in New
York City. This state of affairs offends and dismays
Prince Sihanouk, who has spoken out against both
the D.K. and the PRK at UN meetings.

After the fall of Democratic Kampuchea, Sihanouk settled into a residence provided by the Chinese government in Beijing and started to organize a government-in-exile, just as he had done a decade earlier, after Lon Nol's coup. He founded a group called the National United Front for an Independent, Neutral, Peaceful, and Cooperative Cambodia (FUNCINPEC). Closely related to FUNCINPEC is the Armée Nationale Sihanoukienne (ANS), which is a semimilitary guerrilla force, the fighting arm of FUNCINPEC. Sihanouk employed the by-now-familiar strategies of globe-trotting and speechmaking to drum up international support for FUNCINPEC. He also drew the world's attention to Cambodia's plight by writing several books: *War and Hope: The Case for Cambodia* (1980) and *Memories Sweet and Bitter* (1981). Before long, however, he was once again confronted with a difficult decision: Should he ally himself with what remained of the Khmer Rouge, even though he had distanced himself from the D.K. regime? Bands of Khmer Rouge were still active in Cambodia. Because Pol Pot had disappeared from public view, Khieu Samphan took over as their leader. During the early 1980s, despite their mutual dislike, FUNCINPEC and the Khmer Rouge began to feel that they would have better luck against the PRK if they pooled their strength—as they had done against Lon Nol.

Sihanouk (right) reviews Chinese troops in Beijing in 1983. Chinese forces fought a brief border war against Vietnam soon after the Vietnamese takeover of Cambodia in 1979.

This time, though, there was a third faction to consider. Called the Khmer People's National Liberation Front (KPNLF), it is headed by Son Sann, a follower of Lon Nol who served as prime minister of the Khmer Republic for a time. The KPNLF consists of former members of the Khmer Republic government and army, many of whom had been carrying on guerrilla warfare against the Khmer Rouge since 1975. Like FUNCINPEC and the Khmer Rouge, the KPNLF has opposed the PRK regime from its beginning. Therefore, although the leaders of each of the three anti-PRK groups distrusted each other, they shared a common goal: to rid Cambodia of the Vietnamese-controlled PRK regime.

As early as March 1980, Sihanouk met in Washington, D.C., with Son Sann to discuss the possibilities for cooperation between FUNCINPEC and the KPNLF. Throughout 1981, the prince strove to organize a coalition, or association, of the anti-PRK groups. He was encouraged to do so by his Chinese hosts, who found themselves in the awkward position of wanting to give support to all three groups but being criticized by the other two every time it helped one. China wanted a coalition of the resistance movements so that it would not be expected to favor one over the other two. The resistance leaders, too, recognized that they would be unable to accomplish much without at least a show of cooperation.

In 1982, after many false starts, the members of the Association of South East Asian Nations (ASEAN) persuaded the Khmer Rouge and the two non-Communist resistance groups to negotiate an agreement. As a result, Sihanouk, Khieu Samphan, and Son Sann signed a document that formed the Coalition Government of Democratic Kampuchea, or CGDK. (The use of the name Democratic Kampuchea is a clear signal that the Khmer Rouge is the most powerful of the three resistance groups; Prince Sihanouk has said repeatedly that he rejects the name and wants the country to be called Cambodia again.) China promptly announced that it would support all three factions of the CGDK equally, and the United States and some other na-

Kampuchean guerrillas prepare to engage Vietnamese troops along the Thai-Cambodian border in 1985. The guerrilla forces were made up of three elements, two of them Khmer Rouge, one of them troops loyal to Sihanouk; they fought against Vietnamese troops and the Vietnam-backed government in Phnom Penh.

tions have acknowledged the CGDK as the legitimate representative of Cambodia.

Prince Sihanouk was named president and chief of state of the CGDK; Son Sann became its prime minister and head of government; and Khieu Samphan was named vice-president of foreign affairs. (Pol Pot continued to command the Khmer Rouge army from hiding places in the jungle until 1985, at which time Khieu Samphan announced that Pol Pot had retired to direct something called the Higher Institute for National Defense, of which nothing is known.) The CGDK, however, has never been viewed by its members as a government. It is a purely temporary arrangement, directed toward the single goal of toppling the PRK. Each of the three groups in the CGDK has promised that when that goal is achieved free elections will be held in Cambodia; naturally, each group hopes to win the elections and keep the other two groups out of power. The Khmer Rouge sum up their feelings toward the other resistance groups in the saying "There are three boats crossing the river, but only one will reach the other side." Before any of the boats can reach the other side of the river, though, the PRK government must be unseated.

One of several refugee camps just inside Thailand, home to several hundred thousand Cambodian refugees. Some of the camps are controlled by the Khmer Rouge, others by Sihanouk's forces.

Throughout the 1980s, the resistance forces of the CGDK chipped away at the Vietnamese and PRK armies. In 1983, Vietnam announced that it would maintain a military presence in Cambodia until the threat of invasion from China had disappeared. About 140,000 Vietnamese troops remained in Cambodia for most of the rest of the decade. Finally, in late 1989, under pressure from the United States and the world community to get out of Cambodia, Vietnam withdrew most of its officials and troops, turning the defense of Cambodia's newest regime over to the PRK's own small and ill-trained army.

Each of the three resistance groups has established its own "territories" along Cambodia's borders, places where it administers refugee camps (several hundred thousand Cambodians still live in such camps, awaiting the overthrow of the PRK) and commands the loyalty of the villagers. High-ranking officers of the CGDK, including Prince Sihanouk, occasionally tour the camps. Sihanouk has even been known to lead an entourage of Western journalists and photographers from Bangkok across the

Thai-Cambodian border for a brief photo session in one of his camps, which he describes as "Sihanouk-controlled Cambodian soil." The Khmer Rouge is the largest of the three forces and the ANS is the smallest. Sihanouk, though, remains the most visible — and, to many people around the world — the most acceptable symbol of the resistance movement.

As the border war ground on throughout the 1980s with little sign of approaching victory against the PRK, tension among the member groups of the CGDK increased. Reports from within the country indicated that on many occasions the three resistance forces fought against each other as well as against the Vietnamese and PRK armies. In January 1988, disgusted with the coalition's lack of progress and distrustful of the Khmer Rouge, Sihanouk resigned his post in the CGDK — only to resume it a month later. That same year, at ASEAN-sponsored peace talks in Djakarta, Indonesia, he accused the Khmer Rouge of trying to wipe out the ANS and end popular support for a non-Communist regime.

Soldiers aboard a bus headed from Phnom Penh to Vietnam during the Vietnamese withdrawal from Cambodia in 1989. The Vietnamese pulled out because of international pressure and to ease the burden of the war on their economy. Their departure left the Vietnam-backed Phnom Penh government to fight alone against the Khmer Rouge–Sihanouk guerrillas.

The fragile bond of cooperation between the CGDK members was further strained in 1989, when Vietnam began preparations for withdrawing its troops from Cambodia. Suddenly, the PRK appeared vulnerable. In an effort to shift the balance of power, PRK leaders began suggesting deals to various members of the CGDK.

In May, in an attempt to woo Sihanouk, Hun Sen redesigned the PRK flag to resemble FUNCINPEC's flag and announced that the country's name had been changed to the State of Cambodia. Furthermore, said Hun Sen, Buddhism was being restored as the national religion, laws against private ownership of property were being canceled, and the death penalty was being abolished. All of these moves softened the hard-line approach to government that had been established under direct Vietnamese domination, and it seemed that the PRK might be more flexible than anyone had expected. Hun Sen even stated that he would be willing to acknowledge Prince Sihanouk as Cambodia's head of state.

In response, Sihanouk hinted that he might be willing to return to Phnom Penh to negotiate a peace settlement with the PRK — but without the Khmer Rouge and the KPNLF. The prince met with U.S. vice-president Dan Quayle and told him that the Khmer Rouge could be excluded from a settlement in Cambodia only if the Chinese could be persuaded to abandon them — this conversation seemed to suggest that Sihanouk was seeking U.S. help in disentangling himself from the Communists. But in July 1989, at the International Peace Conference on Cambodia, in Paris, he reversed his position and declared that he would not make a separate deal with the PRK. His change of heart probably came about in part because he fears further antagonizing the Khmer Rouge and in part because Hun Sen's concessions are superficial ones; it is unlikely that the PRK is yet willing to surrender any real power.

At the end of the 1980s, with Vietnam out of Cambodia and the PRK struggling to consolidate its power and fight off the attack of the resistance groups, Sihanouk remains a central figure in Cam-

> *One never knew what Sihanouk actually believed [during the Khmer rebellion of the early 1970s], ensconced in his Peking mansion far from the battles and reality.*
>
> —ELIZABETH BECKER
> American journalist

bodian politics. From his residences in Beijing and Pyongyang, North Korea, he travels constantly, appearing here at an international conference, there at an embassy party, always reminding the world of Cambodia's existence and of its problems.

Although nearly 35 years have passed since he sat on the throne of the god-king and 20 since he governed Cambodia, Sihanouk is a symbol of continuity — a living link between the country's past and its future — to many of the Cambodian people and to the rest of the world. Yet his role in that future is uncertain. If a peace settlement is made, he may find himself shunted into a formal position such as head of state with little or no real power; he may, on the other hand, surprise everyone by rising to the top of the heap again, as he has done so often in his career.

It is to Sihanouk, if to any single person, that Cambodians owe their independence from France, but the generation of Cambodians that has come of age since he fled the country in 1970 associates him more with the brutality of his allies the Khmer Rouge than with the glorious days of newfound independence. Nevertheless, no real settlement will be possible in Cambodia without Sihanouk's participation.

As the 1980s drew to an end, Sihanouk continued to play a central role in Cambodian politics, as he had for almost half a century. But with a new civil war looming on the horizon at the dawn of the 1990s, he and his long-suffering nation faced an uncertain future.

Further Reading

Armstrong, John P. *Sihanouk Speaks.* New York: Walker, 1964.

Becker, Elizabeth. *When the War Was Over: The Voices of Cambodia's Revolution and Its People.* New York: Simon & Schuster, 1987.

Chandler, David. *A History of Cambodia.* Boulder, CO: Westview Press, 1983.

Etcheson, Craig. *The Rise and Demise of Democratic Kampuchea.* Boulder, CO: Westview Press, 1984.

Hildebrand, George, and Gareth Porter. *Cambodia: Starvation and Revolution.* New York: Monthly Review Press, 1976.

Kiernan, Ben. *How Pol Pot Came to Power: A History of Communism in Kampuchea, 1930–1975.* London: Verso, 1985.

Kiernan, Ben, and Chanthou Boua, eds. *Peasants and Politics in Kampuchea, 1942–1981.* Armonk, NY: M. E. Sharpe, 1982.

Mam, Teeda Butt. *To Destroy You Is No Loss: The Odyssey of a Cambodian Family.* New York: Atlantic Monthly Press, 1987.

May, Someth. *Cambodian Witness: An Autobiography of Someth May.* New York: Random House, 1987.

Ngor, Haing, and Roger Warner. *A Cambodian Odyssey.* New York: Warner Books, 1989.

Osborne, Milton E. *Before Kampuchea: Preludes to Tragedy.* Boston: Allen & Unwin, 1984.

Ponchard, Francois. *Cambodia: Year Zero.* Translated by Nancy Amphoux. New York: Holt, Rinehart & Winston, 1978.

Shaplen, Robert. *Bitter Victory.* New York: Harper & Row, 1986.

Shawcross, William. *The Quality of Mercy: Cambodia, Holocaust, and Modern Conscience.* New York: Simon & Schuster, 1984.

Sihanouk, Norodom. *War and Hope: The Case for Cambodia.* Translated by Mary Feeney. New York: Pantheon Books, 1980.

Sihanouk, Norodom, and Wilfred G. Burchett. *My War with the CIA.* London: Penguin Books, 1973.

Steinberg, David J. *Cambodia: Its People, Its Society, Its Culture.* New Haven, CT: HRAF Press, 1959.

Stuart-Fox, Martin. *The Murderous Revolution: Life and Death in Pol Pot's Kampuchea.* New York: Alternative Publishers, 1986.

Chronology

Oct. 31, 1922	Born Prince Samdech Preah Norodom Sihanouk Varman in Phnom Penh, Cambodia, in French Indochina
April 25, 1941	Named king of Cambodia at age 18 by the French
1945	Japanese occupation of Cambodia during World War II ends; Sihanouk declares Cambodia independent of France in March; French control is restored in October
1949	Cambodia becomes an associated state within the French Union; Sihanouk begins the "king's crusade" for full independence
1953	Cambodia receives independence from France
1955	Sihanouk gives up the throne and is elected prime minister; heads Cambodia's government for more than a decade; relations with the United States worsen; war in Vietnam spreads throughout Southeast Asia
1970	Military government headed by General Lon Nol takes control of Cambodia and deposes Sihanouk; Sihanouk forms a government-in-exile in the People's Republic of China
1975	Khmer Rouge (Communist) guerrillas led by Pol Pot overthrow Lon Nol's government and change the country's name to Democratic Kampuchea; Sihanouk returns from exile but is soon placed under house arrest by the Khmer Rouge
Jan. 1979	The Vietnamese army captures Phnom Penh and ends the Khmer Rouge regime; both Pol Pot and Sihanouk flee
1980	Sihanouk denounces the Vietnamese-backed People's Republic of Kampuchea (PRK); vies for leadership among opponents of the PRK
1982	Joins the Lon Nol and Khmer Rouge factions in a coalition that hopes to overthrow the PRK
1989	Vietnam withdraws its troops from Cambodia, leaving the PRK in charge; guerrilla warfare continues among various factions in several provinces; Sihanouk takes part in an international peace conference on Cambodia in Paris

Index

Madhavi Kuckreja has a master's degree in political science from the New School for Social Research in New York City. She has worked at the United Nations, at the National Lawyers Guild, and for Nagarik Ekta Manch (Citizens for Communal Harmony), a human rights and relations organization based in New Delhi, India. She has traveled extensively in Europe, Asia, Australia, and South America.

Arthur M. Schlesinger, jr., taught history at Harvard for many years and is currently Albert Schweitzer Professor of the Humanities at City University of New York. He is the author of numerous highly praised works in American history and has twice been awarded the Pulitzer Prize. He served in the White House as special assistant to Presidents Kennedy and Johnson.

PICTURE CREDITS

AP/Wide World Photos: pp. 12, 14, 17, 36, 37, 38, 39, 40, 41, 44, 45, 49, 50, 51, 52, 54, 57, 59, 61, 63, 68, 71, 72, 75, 78, 80, 83, 84, 85, 89, 90, 92, 93, 94–95, 100, 101, 104; Bettmann: p. 27; Gary Tong (map): p. 24–25; United Nations photo: pp. 2, 20, 22, 23, 28, 30, 73, 79; UPI/Bettmann Newsphotos: pp. 18–19, 32, 35, 42, 47, 56, 65, 67, 77, 81, 86, 88, 91, 97, 98